the Wind Done Gone

ALICE RANDALL

A MARINER BOOK

Houghton Mifflin Company

BOSTON NEW YORK

FIRST MARINER BOOKS EDITION 2002

For information about permission to reproduce selections from this book,
write to Permissions, Houghton Mifflin Harcourt Publishing Company,
215 Park Avenue South, New York, New York 10003

Visit our Web site: www.hmhco.com

Library of Congress Cataloging-in-Publication Data

Randall, Alice.
    The wind done gone / Alice Randall.
        p.   cm.
    ISBN 0-618-10450-x (hc)
    ISBN 0-618-21906-4 (pbk)
    ISBN 978-0-618-21906-3 (pbk)
        1. Afro-American women — Fiction.
    2. Racially mixed people — Fiction.   3. Atlanta
    (Ga.) — Fiction.   I. Title.

    PS3568.A486 W56   2001
    813'.6 — dc21   00-046544

Book design by Anne Chalmers
Fonts used: Granjon, Engravers Gothic BT, Edwardian Script,
Johann Sparkling, Type Embellishments

Printed in the United States of America

DOH 10 9 8 7

This novel is the author's critique of and reaction to the world described
in Margaret Mitchell's *Gone With the Wind*. It is not authorized by the
Stephens Mitchell Trusts, and no sponsorship or endorsement
by the Mitchell Trusts is implied.

THE WIND DONE GONE

NOTES ON THE TEXT

This document was discovered in the early 1990s. It was among the effects of an elderly colored lady who had been in an assisted-living center just outside Atlanta.

The resident's name was Prissy Cynara Brown.

Specifically, two documents were found: a leather-bound diary, written in an ornate and hard-to-decipher hand with a pen and pencil, and a typescript of the diary prepared sometime later.

According to notations in her medical records, Ms. Brown was hospitalized in July of 1936 for a period of three months after suffering a severe emotional collapse. She was hospitalized again for a month in 1940, beginning on New Year's Day. Other than these two episodes (which coincide with the publication and movie première of Margaret Mitchell's *Gone With the Wind*), it appears from letters and clippings that Ms. Brown had enjoyed a life of excellent health and service to the community, frustrated only by her inability to get the diary published.

Pressed into the diary was a photo-postcard of the Washington Monument under construction, a fragment of green silk, and a poem by Ernest Dowson, "Non sum qualis eram bonae sub regno Cynarae."

NON SUM QUALIS ERAM BONAE SUB REGNO CYNARAE*

Last night, ah, yesternight, betwixt her lips and mine
There fell thy shadow, Cynara! thy breath was shed
Upon my soul between the kisses and the wine;
And I was desolate and sick of an old passion,
    Yea, I was desolate and bowed my head:
I have been faithful to thee, Cynara! in my fashion.

All night upon mine heart I felt her warm heart beat,
Night-long within mine arms in love and sleep she lay;
Sure the kisses of her bought red mouth were sweet;
But I was desolate and sick of an old passion,
    When I awoke and found the dawn was gray:
I have been faithful to thee, Cynara! in my fashion.

I have forgot much, Cynara! gone with the wind,
Flung roses, roses riotously with the throng,
Dancing, to put thy pale, lost lilies out of mind;
But I was desolate and sick of an old passion,
    Yea, all the time, because the dance was long:
I have been faithful to thee, Cynara! in my fashion.

I cried for madder music and for stronger wine,
But when the feast is finished and the lamps expire,
Then falls thy shadow, Cynara! the night is thine;
And I am desolate and sick of an old passion,
    Yea, hungry for the lips of my desire:
I have been faithful to thee, Cynara! in my fashion.

—Ernest Dowson, 1867–1900

*I am not as I was under the reign of the good Cynara
—from Horace's *Odes*

THE WIND DONE GONE

1

ℐoday is the anniversary of my birth. I have twenty-eight years. This diary and the pen I am writing with are the best gifts I got—except maybe my cake. R. gave me the diary, the pen, and the white frosted tiers. He also gave me emerald earbobs. I think maybe my emeralds are just green glass; I hope maybe they be genuine peridots.

I was born May 25, 1845, at half-past seven in the morning into slavery on a cotton farm a day's ride from Atlanta. My father, Planter, was the master of the place; my mother was the Mammy. My half-sister, Other, was the belle of five counties. She was not beautiful, but men seldom recognized this, caught up in the cloud of commotion and scent in which she moved. R. certainly didn't; he married her. But then again, he just left her. Maybe that means something to me. Maybe he's just the unseldom one who do recognize.

2

If I strip the flesh off my bones, like they stripped the clothes off my flesh in the slave market down near the battery in Charleston, this would be my skeleton: childhood on a cotton farm; a time of shawl-fetch slavery away in Charleston; a bare-breasted hour on an auction block; drudge slavery as a maid in Beauty's Atlanta brothel, when Milledgeville was the capital of Georgia and Atlanta was nothing; a season of candle-flame concubinage in the attic of that house; a watery Grand Tour of Europe; and, finally, concubinage in my own white clapboard home, with green shutters and gaslights, in the center (near the train depot) of a fast-growing city that has become the capital of Georgia, concubinage that persists till now. How many miles have I traveled to come back to here?

3

They called me Cinnamon because I was skinny as a stick and brown. But my name is Cynara. Now when I tell it, I say they called me Cinnamon because I was sweet and spicy. Sweet, hot, strong, and black — like a good cup of coffee. Leastways, that's how Planter liked his coffee.

Planter used to say I was his cinnamon and Mammy was his coffee.

He said those words a day I had gotten into trouble dashing before Other upon the stained-glass colored light that fell in rows of blue and pink diamonds down the wide hall of the big house. If I was ten years old, it must have been 1855. I bumped into the leg of the Hewitt sideboard. Other was ten years old too. It was one of those days we had back when everything seemed it would always be just as it has always been. Everything and everyone had a place and rested deep in it, or so it seemed that day to would-be knights and ten-year-olds. Then I bumped into that carved leg, and the shell-shaped bonbon dish jumped off Lady's sideboard as if it just wanted to split into a hundred porcelain shards on the lemon-oiled pine floor. Something had changed, and I had changed it. Someone wanted to beat me. Mammy said she'd beat me good, with a belt. Other lied and said *she'd* knocked into the table. Said it 'cause she knew it would pain Mammy to give me a whipping.

And sometimes Planter said it when he heard me making up little rhymes to sing to myself. Sometimes when Mammy was putting Other to sleep on a day pallet for a nap, he would call for me to sit at his feet on the broad porch and sing my little songs to him. "Cindy, come sing, come sing! Ain't you my Cinnamon and she my coffee?" he'd ask. And I'd be slow to go, because I knew someone might be missing me.

On the day Planter told me I was leaving the place, I asked him what he had meant when he said that I was his cinnamon and she was his coffee. He said to me, "I mean a man can do without his cinnamon but he can't do without his coffee." I poked my lip out. "I mean you're a gracious plenty."

"I belong here?"

"Gracious plenty foreign to me child."

R. says Planter was an Irishman and all Irish are shiftless, lazy crackers, no matter how rich they get. He always wants me to look outside the neighborhood for models of my deportment. He often mentions that Georgia was once a penal colony. The first time he said it, I didn't know what a "penal colony" was. He says only the English and the French know anything about gracious plenty. He says when Planter and Mammy got together, they cooked a broth too rich for potato-water blood.

It was Planter who sent me away, but he got the go-ahead from Mama. It was the year his third son died, and he said it would be a good turn for me. I was thirteen the day they rode me off. It was 1858.

Mammy was my Mama. Even though she let me go, I miss her. I miss her every time I look into a mirror and see her eyes. Sometimes I comb through my long springy curls and pretend that the hand holding the comb is hers.

But I don't know what that looks like. Then I wish I was Other, the girl whose sausage curls I've seen Mammy comb and comb. I wish for the tight kinks of the comber or the glossy sausages of the combed. I wish not to be out of the picture.

Mammy always called me Chile. She never called me soft or to her softness. She called me to do things, usually for Other, who she called Lamb. It was "Get dressed, Chile!" and "What's mah Lamb gwanna wear?"

4

I have tried to forget the place I was sent from, Cotton Farm, and the house in which I was born, Tata. If Sherman had burned it down to the ground, I believe I would not have labored in vain. I believe I would have succeeded. I believe I might have attained my own personal succession. But he didn't. And I keep thinking that God saved it for some purpose, but it wasn't God who saved Cotton Farm; it was Garlic, when he flapped like a fool and begged the Union troops to carry him away from all the fever and dying in the house. Every time he'd approach a Union horse and rider, they'd buck back farther away. Nobody wanted to get close enough to any of the buildings to rescue a slave or make a "building barbecue" possible. So, after all that I have forgotten, I still remember the place. The place, and the people who sent me away.

5

They called her Mammy. Always. Some ways I like that. Some days when it was kind of like we—she and me—had a secret against them, the planting people, I like it. Different days, when it feels she wasn't big enough to have a name, I hate it. I heard tell down the years they compared her to an elephant. They shouted down to their ancestors: She was big as an elephant with tiny dark round eyes. But she wasn't big enough to own a name. To me she was big as a house. Big as two houses. I'd be scared to be that.

Scared to be bigger than a minute and a snap of dark fingers. "She's no bigger than a minute," Mammy would say, snapping her thick, strong-as-branches fingers, stealing words from him whose watch Garlic inherited. Him who was my Daddy and never gave her or me nothing like time, Planter.

Anyways, Mammy's eyes are big, just like mine. Garlic used to tell me that all the time. Garlic was Planter's valet, and he liked women with great big legs. If I ever started to get big, R. would let me go.

Even Other called Mammy out of her name. Other, who loved my mother; Other, who ran to her Mammy like I never seen nobody run to anybody, or anything, for the more significant matter, ran to Mammy like she was couch and pillow, blanket and mattress, prayer and God. Other rested her head on Mammy's brown pillow breasts, snuggled in beneath a blanket of fat brown arm, breathed in the prayer of Mammy's breath and out the god of her presence, never came to know there was any reason to give Mammy Planter's watch. So Garlic got it. Garlic wears it. Other owns Mother by more than ink and law.

6

This is my book. If I die tomorrow, nobody'll remember me except maybe somebody who find this book. I read *Uncle Tom's Cabin*. I didn't see me in it. Uncle Tom sounded just like Jesus to me, in costume. I don't want to go in disguise. I don't want to write no novel. I'm just afraid of forgetting. I don't talk to anybody save Beauty and a few folks, so nobody remembers what I am thinking. If I forget my real name, won't be anybody to tell it to me. No one here knows. I'm going to write down everything. Something like Mr. Frederick Douglass.

———

R. visits my house more now, much more than he did before he quit Other. These days the sun sets with him sitting on my long wide porch turned toward the sideyard. Many nights now, he sleeps here. He says, "I love this house." I say, "You designed it." I don't say, "And you paid for it," but that's another reason to love a thing. He says, "It's quieter than the other house." He doesn't speak her name. The architecture of my home is a bow to R. and what he remembers of the houses of Charleston. I don't want to remember anything of Charleston at all, but the houses were cool, and R. wouldn't approve a cupola for the hot air to rise into, so I have turned my house away from the street.

It's a pity my street sees only the short side of me. It's a lovely brown street that didn't exist, even in dreams, before the war. There's a new church for the colored, First Congregational, a colored druggist, colored grocers, colored undertakers, colored schoolteachers down from Canada. Thanks to white women who want to improve the lot of what they are always calling "our children," R. is not, when he stays over, the street's only white resident. And I'm not sure how long he will be its only millionaire. There's a dusky man lives on this road who sells insurance. Many folk believe that man will someday soon be a millionaire. And there's more than one university for colored people springing up. With R. here more, I miss some of the neighborhood gossip, but I catch some from across town. There's a drink like something a root doctor would make, dark, with bubbles all sugared up to keep the swamp taste down, and the white folk are paying plenty pretty money to drink it. I've never tasted it. Only white folk go into the pharmacy where they sell it. R. says he's going to bring me a taste.

7

I almost never hear from Cotton Farm. More and more rarely someone will stop by my kitchen window and call, "Homefolks say hey." They can't write, and I don't expect them to. So when the letter came, I was afraid of tearing its seal.

Mammy is dying and she want me to come home before she go. I ain't saying yes, and I ain't saying no. I'm saying, I ain't stood on Cotton Farm since I was still saying *ain't,* and I don't know if I want to go back there.

Mammy is dying surrounded by homefolks. I got no feet to take me there. Mammy is dying and I don't want to go home. No more than she ever wanted to come see me under this fine roof. Mammy is dying and I want to touch her but I don't want her to touch me.

I'm going to die one day; this is telling me that. When I was a girl, I say to myself, "I won't hold you when your hair turn gray and your skin turn gray, when your eyes glaze over blue like old folks' eyes do. I won't make a pillow for your head. I seen rheumy eyes like hardboiled eggs, deep green circles glazed over white, and I think those will be your eyes one day. I won't hold you and I will never eat eggs again." Like a prayer of protection I said those things, and now it is not the threat I meant it to be. It's just a prescient prophecy, just a curse on me.

Mammy, Mama, I have no more idea how to hold you old than you had how to hold me young. All I got is ambition to love you more than you loved me.

8

*L*ast night I dreamed of Cotton Farm.

I was serving at table, pulling the silken cord of the shoofly as guests dined, as they spoke of shopping in New Orleans, of buying furniture, and wallpaper, and silver. As they ate Mammy's dinner, I pulled the cord again and again; the cord pulled the silk brocade flap cantilevered above the table and fanned the guests from Savannah and Annapolis. As I performed my duty, I heard planters speak of turning cotton into silver. Someone pronounced "alchemy of slavery," and a shining coffeepot, candlesticks, and saltcellars changed before my dreaming eyes into little piles of cotton balls flecked with seed. Then I looked at my arms, and they changed too. The two golden brown little hills, one in the top of each of my arms, grew into little mountains as I pulled the cord and Mammy smiled, passing the green beans.

As I continued to fan and the guests continued to eat, Other appeared at the table, and the wallpaper began to move. In my dream, just as in life, the dining room wallpaper is painted all over with the story of Telemachus, in the land of the enchantress Calypso, searching for his father, Odysseus. Garlic once told me he had seen paper just like it in the home of President Jackson. I didn't believe him. Presidents don't invite folk like Planter to dinner. At eleven I'd seen enough of "the quality" to know that. But I liked his story. And in life I liked the wallpaper. In my dream it wouldn't stop moving, and I started to hate it. Didn't I know what it was like to live in the land of an enchantress and to long for your father?

My eyes turned from the wallpaper to the windows, my arm still pulling, still fanning. There were many windows. The house was built to let the outside in, the fragrance of peach and plum, the outside light after it is tinted by the colored glass of the windows. But I am inside looking out, toward the distant cabins.

Through the pink glass I see black smoke from a cabin chimney. I see into the cabin itself: I see a baby gently rocked in the arms of her mother.

ALICE RANDALL

I am still fanning as my mother serves Other a choice piece of dark meat. There is a painted porcelain bonbon dish on the sideboard behind them. It falls from the sideboard and shatters. Over and over it falls. And I keep fanning.

I wake up screaming. R. says, Strong meat tastes sweet.

9

If I go back there, I'm going to get my Daddy's watch and have it engraved to read, TO R.B. FROM M.E. I don't feel like laughing, but I can just see R. laughing at my joke. I can just see him open the satin-lined leather box. He'll understand; he expects me to play with letters. He taught me how to read in bed. I praised him for it. His stomach was my first paper, lip rouge was my pencil, and the cleaning rag was my tongue. We learned me well. R. gave me the tools. I learned to write, right on his belly.

He's used to buying women and ladies and buying them jewelry. I'm going to give him some of his own back. I like to give R. things. I like to give him what he's used to paying for.

Sometimes when we are in bed and he's sucking on one of my breast, pulling hard and steady so the pull only

· 12 ·

brings me the pleasure, sometimes when he's nursing on me, I smile, because he can't get what he wants here. I'm dry. But I let him suck himself to sleep. And sometimes there comes over his face a look of peace. Sometimes when I'm riding astride him and my gals dangle toward his face, he snaps at them like the foxes snapping at grapes dangling just above their mouths, and I laugh. Once, just after that, he pushed so hard into me that something broke inside and we were touching without anything between us, like a fever came over me, and he had the same sickness. Then I closed my eyes and I saw Other.

She was old enough to walk. She walked right past me, past Lady, she walked right past Lady and me, over to Mammy, reached up for Mammy, and my Mama reached down to pull Other up onto her hip. Other reached into the top of Mammy's dress and pulled out my mother's breast. "I want some titty-tip," she said, and I ached in some place I didn't know I had, where my heart should have been but wasn't. I've come to believe that was the very first time I ever felt my soul, and it was having a spasm. It clinched again, pushing the air out of me in a hiccup. I flushed in a rage of possession as those little white hands drew the nipple toward the little pink mouth, then clasped on.

I turned to see the delicate Lady. She was clutching at her cinched waist and staggering back. I ran toward her;

she steadied herself, using my head as a kind of crutch or prop. I started fanning the flies off her and I kept fanning.

Wasn't it then Planter walked out on the whitewashed porch and smiled? Did he say, "My peculiar heaven, my peculiar, particular heaven"? I believe that's what he said. That's what he says when I remember it. His frail wife near faints and is fanned by the fairest of pretty pickaninnies, M.E., and he's pronouncing, "My peculiar heaven."

The rosebud mouth attached to the black moon in the brown breast, the curving back of the loving woman lifting the child to her pleasures, as the child, awake, untouched by stays and hoops, stands on tippy-toe to get her fill of pleasure, all raven-haired and unashamed of hunger. Him laughed. For his first-born daughter the pangs of hunger were as delightful as a mosquito bite, something to scratch in the next moment, the promise of pleasure to come.

He didn't see me hiding behind Lady's skirts or see the look Mammy gave me over Other's head. Planter only saw his daughter taking pleasure where he himself had done.

10

Now I'm grown, I wonder what Lady saw. She was just the oldest child on the porch, seventeen, with a three-year-old daughter. Never certain of feeding, I did not welcome hunger. I looked and wanted to suck; Lady looked and wanted to suckle-feed. We were both envious.

Later, when it looked like the four o'clock flowers opened their faces to the sun, but really when they smiled their relief to the arriving shade, when the baby of the house, Other, slept on a cool soft pallet and I tried to sleep on a hot rug in the kitchen, Lady called for a basin of water and a glass of sweet milk, and I was roused to serve it.

Or was it when Other was napping on a pallet in her room and I was one of the children fanning the flies away from little Miss while she slept, that Lady called from the next room, "Mammy, send Cindy up with some cool water and a glass of sweet milk. I'm thirsty and I want a sponge bath." I walked in with what she wanted. Lady made herself comfortable in her rocking chair. "Are you hungry?" I nodded. She handed me the glass of milk. I hesitated. "You can drink it." I took the glass and drank. She took the glass from my hand and drank right after me. I was surprised. Really I was astounded. I didn't know the word then, but that's what I was.

"Help me unbutton my dress; I want to wash." I helped her take off her dress. Her bared breast was just a little thing with a dented nipple almost as big as the circle it stood in. The circle was that tiny. "Are you still hungry?" I nodded again.

She pulled me onto her lap and I suckled at her breast till her warm milk filled me. As always, it was a cheering surprise for both of us. We had been sharing these little spurred-by-envy suppers all my memory, but each time the milk came and how long it came without running out was a mystery to us both. Later, when I slept beside her, she said, "You're my little girl, aren't you?"

11

*M*ammy worked from can't-see in the morning to can't-see at night, in that great whitewashed wide-columned house surrounded by curvy furrowed fields. The mud, the dirt, was so red, when you looked at the cotton blooming in a field it brought to mind a sleeping gown after childbirth—all soft white cotton and blood.

If it was mine to be able to paint pictures, if I possessed the gift of painting, I would paint a cotton gown balled up and thrown into a corner waiting to be washed, and I would call it "Georgia."

Mammy never knew rest, but she is no fool. I believe she knows why R. doesn't give a damn about Other anymore. Mammy knows that he's in love with me, and after the Tragedy there's nothing to keep us apart.

The Tragedy, yes, that is what it was. I cried when that child died. R. thought she was beautiful, and Other thought she was spoilt. Neither one of them was right. Everything that was gold and bold lived big in Precious. She looked too much like my Daddy to be pretty. Except when she kissed me and I would pull her curls. Precious: that's what I called her. Her grandfather would look right through me, but she would run to me and throw her arms around my waist. I got his hugs from her, and they were sweet to me, precious. She gave me my Daddy's kisses. She was his grandchild and they were my kisses, and her mouth looked just like his mouth. Not like Other's or Lady's or R.'s. She had Planter's mouth, and she gave me Planter's kisses.

The night Precious died, R. tried to plant a child in me. Most every other time, he pulled out, making a mess on my belly that shamed me. He didn't want any bastards, beige or white.

They thought he stayed alone with her, his dead Precious, in that room those days between her death and the burial. But I was there. I was there. I held his hand in the burning light, because Precious was afraid of the dark.

In that room we were a family. Grief will form one

family just the way it will destroy another. It's a primary force. What did he lose when he lost her? What do I know 'bout what runs between a daddy and his daughter? Not very much. R. didn't know why Precious cried in the dark, and I don't know either.

12

Georgia is dirty laundry what needs washing.

I told that to R. last evening. We were out walking in Oakland Cemetery. Oakland Cemetery may well be the prettiest garden in Atlanta. And the dead don't care who's out walking with who and if their colors match. Plenty folks, black and white, pack picnics and make a feast of a visit. All those gravestones got us to talking 'bout whether I should or should not run home to Mammy.

I have my reasons for not going and I have his. His reason is Other. Chivalry dictates that his wife and his mistress do not meet. I said, "Georgia is laundry what needs washing." He put one of his manicured hands over each of my ears and pressed. "Peanut head," he said. I couldn't tell if it was a joke or an insult, he was pressing so hard. I didn't like the fact he wouldn't acknowledge my truth.

Georgia is dirty laundry what needs washing.

If I didn't want to back down, I knew I had to turn my taunt into a joke. "I've got a big head. A watermelon head, more likely. Too big for ladies' hats. At least a walnut. You can crack open a peanut, so easy," I said. "You can do it with your fingers."

"You're too smart for your own good."

I smiled; he dropped his hands to his side. "I sent you on that Grand Tour as a jest," he said.

I wasn't smiling anymore. "Charleston's dirty laundry too. All of South Carolina." No sooner than I said it, he slapped me. He had never hit me before. No man had.

"The only thing you can beat out of me is my love for you." Beauty taught us to say that, and say it quick. It was the first sentence she taught every girl in her house. It stopped a lot of fights; it stopped her from having to shoot a man or two. It was an easy sentence to remember and a hard sentence to forget, especially with a palm print on your face. Anyway, it wasn't me he wanted to slap. But he couldn't slap Other. "I ain't taking her licks," I said.

I walked away from him. The red imprint of his hand was raised across my cheek. I traced the outline of it with the tip of my finger. Mammy had slapped me too many times to count. I knew well this vanishing brand. Invisible but searing.

Strange how you bring things to you. I think of the

white house and Mammy, and I get slapped. Just what I was afraid of happened before I could even go home. How strange that just when I might go, Other had got there first. Run back to the house because R. left her. I had asked him to tell me what he said, what she said, how it looked, a dozen times. He didn't tell me anything. He only told me it was over.

But the walls have ears, and her maid told my maid, and my maid told me, that Other had run back from Mealy Mouth's deathbed to find R. already packed. That she had declared her love and pleaded with him. That he had cursed her but called her *my darling* or *dear,* but he told her he didn't give a tinker's damn what happened to her. When he walked out, she sat down on the stairs and cried. Then she ran home to my mother. That was just a month ago.

13

I will go to see Beauty today. I met R. under her whorehouse roof. Simple as that. I was fourteen years old. It was just before the war. Beauty needed a maid to pick up after her girls, so she bought me in the slave market down on the water in Charleston. I had an answer when any blue-blooded gentleboy at Beauty's would ask, "How a fine piece of embroidery like you get beyond white columns and painted walls?" They didn't expect an answer, but I had one. A fancy sentence I had practiced to show I was somebody: "A strange series of deaths in rapid succession following an influenza epidemic left a trail of inheritances that led me to the flesh market with a stop of work with a family who couldn't afford to keep a second ladies' maid." My twenty-dollar sentence was usually good for a laugh and a nickel tip.

Truth was, everybody was too busy nursing the sick, mourning, and grieving to write Planter and tell him that his old friend was dead, that the friend's son had died before he could marry, that I was living with a family who needed money, and would he like to buy me back. I didn't know how to write then; I couldn't tell the news that might have saved me.

Beauty bought me to serve in her place as a girl-of-all-work, but there was so much dirty laundry, all I ever did is wash soiled sheets, bleach sheets, iron sheets. You paid for pussy at Beauty's or you didn't get any, and the planters that came to Beauty didn't need to pay for poontang they could steal back at home, so I was most usually the only *female* virgin in the house. Males of that persuasion were frequent visitors. Mainly the planters liked their meat what we liked to call pink—before a girl began to bleed. They had less brats around the place that way. I think Beauty thought of buying me because she wanted to feel like more of a lady to R.

I'm going to stop writing and go right now.

14

*W*alking to Beauty's, my face still stung where R. slapped me. But his words had stung me more. My Grand Tour was rivers: the Thames, the Seine, what do they call all those canals in Venice? What name did that water go by? What destinations were in that book, *Murray's Infallible Handbook*? Rivers and the lake at Como. Atlanta is a landlocked place, a rail terminus, really and only. If it becomes a great city, it will be one of the first not built on a river. I ain't seen a big body of water in a time, but I still have my memories. Something that I cherish so much cannot have been a joke.

I went in a party of some friends of R.'s, an unpaid but working companion. The kind that holds the chairs on deck, fetches games, takes the smallest slice of beef, eats in the cabin when there is no space at table, ate at table when I wasn't hungry when someone needed a companion. I saw paintings. In Rome I met a colored woman from the United States who lived there as a sculptor of marble. She carved marble fauns. She and those rivers were a revelation to me.

Today, I came up the back way and in the kitchen door. Beauty's unpowdered nose was inside a great big cup of coffee. I've seen folk go down to the river to get baptized and I've seen them get sprinkled. None ever seemed so washed as Beauty after her coffee. Each and every morning that old whore jumped fully into that big black cup of coffee, and when she stepped away from her morning meal, she was fully cleansed of the sins of the night.

She didn't wait for Sunday for communion and she didn't wait for the river to be baptized; she had baptism and communion right there in her kitchen every morning. When any of the girls woke themselves up to share breakfast with Beauty, they got communion too. Morning with Beauty was its own religion.

Beauty isn't young. Her face was painted white, and the hair on the top of her head was the same shade of burgundy as the velvet of her front room chairs. Shaped like an hourglass but built like a brick house, she counted the change right the first time. She had a son didn't live with her. She sent him away to school. I don't believe in that. Over the years I've tried to talk Beauty into bringing the boy back with her to live. But she wouldn't hear me. Anyhow, he's a man now.

I sat myself down in the chair beside her. There was an

empty cup in front of me like she was expecting somebody. She poured coffee into it. I asked her what I should
do 'bout going home. Beauty just grunted, but she was
serving me, and that said something. I pulled in closer to
the table. The cup tingled in my hands. Beauty took another sip of coffee. "One way of seeing it, when you got a
bitch for a mother she should expect to die alone. Other
is, blood is blood." It was my turn to grunt. I looked into
her eyes and knew that she expected to die alone. And I
knew that for all her hospitality to me, her absence from
He, him, her son, maybe had earned that. This whore
had no "heart of gold," but then again she didn't pretend
to. She was no better than she should be, but she was as
good as need be. And my need be great.

The hand that had itched to slap her was brushed by
her hand serving me. I tried to remember Mama pouring
me a cup of coffee. Nothing came. She asked me if I was
afraid of going. I said yes. She shook her head. I'd never
seen her pity me. Not when she bought me off the auction block, not when she had me serving for her. She said,
"Sometimes the only way to stop being afraid of a thing is
to let it happen."

Blood is blood. I tried to imagine Other's hand pouring coffee for me. I winced and hoped R.'s bastard was
growing in my belly. Beauty reached out and lifted up
my face with the knuckles of her bent fingers. "If he had
the reason, he might marry you."

"I don't want to give him a reason," I lied.

Lying brings a nervous tickle to my throat. My throat started tickling, and I laughed. Dark brown liquid shot from my mouth onto Beauty. I gasped and coughed again. She pushed me away from the table and all her fine linens. "You gone straight crazy, took the Black Diamond Express. Makes no stops and arrives in hell early." I was trying to stop laughing. I was trying to remember Mammy serving me something, pouring one cup of coffee, but all I could remember was Mammy pouring coffee for Other, her fine white hands trembling as Mammy filled her cup. And Lady holding out the cool glass of fresh milk to me. I don't know what face I made. But Beauty got to looking kinda scared. "Whatever you're thinking about don't think about."

"Then let me pour the next cup of coffee," I said.

15

R. makes "his rounds," as he names them, calling on the mayor, his bankers, hearing the chatter of the town, holding a cracked-kid-gloved finger up to the battering winds of cash, color, and politics each morning, returning to me at noon for his dinner. That's every day.

I have no appetite for presiding in my dining room. Most days I give everybody a holiday. His servants, my friends. There are no silent brown ghosts in this house— there's an eye for every hand and more ears than fingers 'round most houses. How the white people live surrounded by spies, I don't know. I can't do it. The slime of hatred on every sliver of soap, every sheet smoothed across every bed. "Our house has the supreme elegance of privacy," he says, referring to the small number of servants.

It unsettles R. that I chose to build my house in the middle of the colored—he would say "section," I will write "community." He would rather I had built on some outskirt, someplace that wasn't yet a neighborhood to be known as white or colored. But I like to be able to walk places, to church, to the dry goods, to Beauty's.

Most days I cook. It gives me something to do. But we have a cook, Portia Dred. She chose the name from the stories I told her, from the books in my library. The Act of March 2, 1867, debated over many a joint of Mrs. Dred's beef, created three categories of voters for the state and the primary categories of guests for my table: Negroes loyal to the Union who had never been in jail and had lived in the state a year, preferably those who are making money; Yankees poured down from the North finally resident a year, preferably those minting money; and loyal white Southern citizens who had been here forever but were willing to lie and spout the "ironclad oath," preferably those who have hidden money.

I have two books of recipes, and most all the time I cook from them. Almost always if we eat alone. But yesterday I made Mammy's chicken croquettes and fresh smashed peas from memory.

I'm still deciding when and if I will return to Cotton Farm. She, Other, is still in residence there. If I go, I will have to share both the place and Mama with her. I am hoping for a letter saying Mammy's turned the corner.

R. doesn't see my thoughts. They are made too small by his own. He loves Mammy, but not when he thinks of her as my Mama; he loves her through Other. He doesn't choose to remember I have a mother. I choose to forgive R. for what cannot be expected of him.

When we moved into this house, he carried me in his arms through the door and up the stairs into the most beautiful bedroom I had ever seen. When he was making the bed mine, between kisses he said, "Forget everything before now." Over and over he said it. He kissed me so hard. It was the only time he ever begged me. He was on his knees, I was laying on the bed, and he said, "Don't bring your past into this house." But it's breaking in like a robber in the night, and he won't wake up to save me from it, and I don't know if he got a gun anymore would do it. Every day it gets harder to see why he can bring his history into my house, but I can't bring my past. And every day I'm more afraid of my past than I was the day before.

I asked Cook to make the supper. I will try hard to give him what he has begged for, for his sake and my own.

We were served at eight. We began with shrimp étouffé and ended with little pots de crème au chocolat. I wore my Turkish trousers. After dinner, when we were still seated at the dining table, R. tells me what he didn't tell me at noon.

There's a man coming through Atlanta he wants me to meet. I tell him it's not the time, and he smiles in relief. He thinks I'm protecting him from those who would distract him from grief. But then he says we really must have the dinner and I am the one to give it. He flatters me by claiming the superiority of my table — "Never one flavor too many, never one flavor too few" — and I like it. I reward him with an invitation to take a rest with me on the green velvet couch.

He pulls me to him, out of my chair into his lap. Then he waits. I trace his lips with the tip of one of my fingers, then I push the finger into his mouth. When I try to pull it out, his lips tug hard. The tug is familiar. It steadies me. He's looking at me differently now. What the difference is, I don't know. But I see it. He looks at me hard. I raise my eyebrows. I know better than to speak. He says nothing. He just kisses me and looks at my hand as if it was something foreign.

There's a low wide couch in my bedroom upholstered in green velvet. He loves it when I'm sweet to him on it. I feel it calling to us now. When I was young I would invite him by saying, "The morning dew is on the southern lawn," and he would laugh at the proper way I invited him to impropriety. I was barely out of my childhood, just fifteen, when he asked, "Is the little bird twittering in its nest?"

"You make it sound so pretty."

"If you could see what I see." He kissed the lips he could kiss and still let me keep up mumbling proper-sounding improprieties: "The morning dew is on the southern lawn."

There are certain things we do only on that couch. He calls it visiting the honeysuckle garden. When I was old enough to walk, they put a fan in my hand to shoo the flies off Lady. I seen children play. Colored and white—colored far from the house, in the fields. Other, every-where, under tables, in her room. I had no place to play then. My body became my place to play. I became my own playing ground.

Afterward we lie on that couch and talk, his feet propped on my shoulders, my feet propped on his, and I feel braided together. We talk little things, plans for the week, plans for the month, when he will be out of town, how much money I need, how much is left in my account.

He put the heavy string of pearls around my neck. They didn't come from the jewelry store new; they came from the place where you sell things when you need money. A pawn shop. They hang so low, they spill between my breasts, like the foam on fast-running water, a stream of rough white water pouring down onto my belly. I took the edge of the loop that dipped toward my navel and pulled it over his head. We were both encircled in his gold-clasped loop.

Against the smooth gold whiteness of the pearls, the skin of his neck looked yellow, cross-hatched like a dusty yard across which chickens had scratched. He smiled, and there were more lines. I could smell tobacco, coffee, and the shrimp on his tongue. Sometimes I was shrimp and he was the shrimpy taste of me on his tongue. Sometimes he was a pirate and life was a still salty basin of water just off a strand of sand. Sometimes it feels good, sometimes feeling good is enough. Sometimes I don't remember nothing 'cept being a fresh boiled shrimp between his teeth, swallowed but not devoured in the hours when it seemed that I was born to be no more than a taste on his tongue.

I close my eyes but I don't fall asleep. I still have hunger.

When he thought I had fallen asleep, he tiptoed out of

the room, down the front steps, and out the back door of the house he bought for me. He goes to sleep in what he calls his closet, a small apartment in one of the four hundred buildings that survived the fires of the war, a fine old address.

16

I have never forgiven Mammy for the hours I stood bare-breasted in the market in Charleston. I don't know how to forgive her and love myself. After the paste peace of forgetting, she calls to me and I remember. Forgetting is to forgiving as glass is to a diamond, mockingbird. If that golden ring turns brass, Daddy's going to buy you a looking glass, mockingbird.

Bits and pieces. It comes back to me that way. I had a dream last night I was a girl again. In my dreams I am a girl again. I am sent to the market with a heavy load of rice. A little of the rice seeps out. I notice a fine little trail behind me. I panic. I put down my burden, tie a knot in the hole. I am scared. I know I am not still carrying everything. I am exhausted. I lift my burden with grave trepidation and discover it is lighter. After that I started dropping things on purpose. Bits and pieces. Stuff to carry (a chair, a watch, a sack of rice). I unburden myself over the stretch of the time road, arriving at my destination empty.

I always wake up before I arrive, 'cause I know I'd be punished for losing stuff. Sometimes halfway through I put everything down, I untie the shawl, and search for something in the bundle, something both worthy of saving and within my ability to save. Something that's both light and valuable, something I can hold on to when I drop other things. But nothing small enough to carry seems valuable enough to save. I tie up the bundle and try again to carry it all, finding again that everything gets jettisoned along the way.

Last night the dream was different. The people who awaited my bundle—to whom my bundle belonged—were waiting. I could hear their voices just beyond the woods. My parcel was empty. It got colder, so I drew the shawl around me. I wanted to turn back, but I didn't know the way. I start down one road; it looks familiar. I start down another, then another. I return to the first, when I come across a little chair, the last thing I had jettisoned. I start following bits and pieces back to where I had begun. I take the shawl from around my shoulders and begin to make again the package I had jettisoned, even as I shiver.

When I awoke from this dream, I made my way to Beauty's. I didn't dress first; I just threw on a wrapper and went. She was very deep into her cup. One of her girls shared it with her but vanished when I appeared. I told Beauty my dream. She asked me if I knew what it meant. I shook my head no. She took my hands in hers. She took a ring off of her finger; it was big and green like an emerald but it was what she called a peridot. That's how I knew about my earbobs. She slipped the ring on my finger. "I'm not going to tell you where it comes from. I'm just going to tell you that it's yours."

"Where was the ring when I was looking through the shawl?"

"On my hand."

"I can't take this."

"You can't take it, or steal it, or earn it. But I can gift it to you. You can't pour all your water on a table and then have a cup to drink. I'll be your cup."

The stoned weighed on my finger. A tiny slowness of hands. I kissed Beauty on the lips. She kissed me back, and a bit of her powder came off on my cheek. Her paint dabbed my lip. She wiped the stain off my mouth. "Your dream 'minds me of Hansel and Gretel."

"You the witch or the grandmother?"

Beauty looked surprised. "Baby, I'm Hansel."

Hansel play-acting grandma. I laughed all the way home, but my throat didn't tickle. I look after the girl what had just left. I didn't know much more about Beauty than these new girls did. I knew exactly what she was saying. Girls will be girls. The men would leave and we'd crawl into bed together like kittens, scratching, pawing, tumbling into sleep.

17

We were in Venice at the time of the revels before Lent. I went into the plaza wearing a mask and hood. I saw a pretty girl, dark skin, dark eyes. She smelled strong of fish and capers and fried artichokes. I kissed her for Beauty's sake. For Lady's sake. Behind the veil of the mask, in the old Jewish Quarter, I kissed her, kissed her, and didn't cry, because I know one day I will die. And I will not rise again.

18

I leave for Cotton Farm this afternoon. R. has hired a carriage to take me there. I can't go there in his. Cotton Farm. R. fought and tried to die in a Confederate uniform to save this place. I have tried to forget this, but I remember.

19

On the road to Cotton Farm, I carry the same copy of the same letter back to the farm as I carried away from it. It's been with me all these seventeen years.

It's a pissed bed on a cold night to read words on paper saying your name and a price, to read the letters that say you are owned, or to read words that say this one or that one will pay so much money for you to be recaptured. It be better never to read than to read that page with your name on it. There are not that many people who can read who have read those kind of words written about themselves, so you won't know it, won't be known, if I don't tell it. And I ain't gonna tell it, 'cause I don't want any more folks to know. After some of the things I've read, I know if God had loved me, I'd a been born blind. They say Harriet Tubman can't read a lick, and she the black Moses. If not reading didn't help her keep walking on water, surely reading, what there was for her to read, would have sunk her!

I copied it out. The letter Planter wrote. I couldn't read a word of it that day. I came to know what it said before I knew how to read it. It was not an easy text. I didn't come to know its meaning all at once. I had to study on it. First, I couldn't decipher some of the words; then I didn't know what some of the words meant, didn't know the deep meaning of some of the words I knew. When R. finished teaching me, I understood every syllable and I memorized all the sounds.

Dear Thomas,

I hope this letter finds you prospering. Around here, prices and cotton are high, trouble and weeds are low—and you've got rice on top of the cotton unless the malaria rolls through your parts as it does some years, leaving whole acres of slaves dead in the swamps—you should see a fine profit this year. I have a fancy girl I want to settle on you, at a price, a good price. Her name is Cindy.

This is a delicate situation, a delicate situation I know you will understand. The girl is no longer a child and she's getting in the way of our Mammy's work. A matter of divided loyalties. My eldest daughter adores her Mammy; she's beginning to find her Mammy's daughter tiresome. But I have a certain tender concern for this child. To put it clearly, I would not like to see someone who looked so much like my sainted mother ill-used in field or bed. I hope you will take her into your house as a lady's companion. Let her comb your lady's hair, let her wash your lady's silks, and when your son is married, she can be your wedding gift to the new bride and groom. Your boy is spirited and intelligent; he'll manage the thing right.

In her day to come, Cindy will be a trusted Mammy in your great house, which I know you will let your son and daughter-in-law inherit. I will sell you the girl for a dollar. In consideration of the low price I am asking and the value offered, please keep her in shoes and simple fabric for dresses. Feed her well and use her kindly. If you, or any of your sons, ever have a little bloom that needs planting out of the neighborhood, please write. In particular, I wouldn't mind settling a little of your eldest son's property (the progeny of my girl) on my place, if it's a convenience to you.

Twice I've been kilt by a man. Once was when I read Planter's words on paper. At the end of every day Planter counted his money, his acres, and his slaves. All that counted were the acres. And these are the acres to which I return.

20

*I*t almost takes my breath away, Cotton Farm rising from the mists.

21

*M*ammy died two hours before I arrived. They say waiting on me to come kept her living so long. She was about sixty years old. Now I'm near to thirty and she'd be the age of the century when the war came. Sixty-five. 1865. I'm just writing sums because I don't know what to write and I don't want to think.

She expected me up to the end. She died sitting in a chair facing the door. She was rocking, watching the door when it opened. She croaked my name and didn't even bother to draw her last breath. She died with a look of triumph on her face and a sweet ham in her oven. She thought it was me. But it was just Miss Priss, wearing one of Other's cast-off dresses. Why she wanted to put it on, I don't know. The visiting colored preacher pronounced Mammy dead and took the ham home to his children. No one in the old house wanted to eat it.

I need to put down this pen and stop writing for me. I need to put down this pen and send a letter to R. before Other does. I want him to hear the news from me. Every time Mammy wrote to me, someone heard my news first. She had to tell somebody, and they had to write it down. I always hoped it was them that left out the words I wanted to hear. Them and not her. I want to lay down with the body. Drape me over the mass of her.

It's a long road from where I live to Cotton Farm. And every one I have driven it with is dead. Dead, with one remaining to be buried. I want to sop up the heat from her body.

22

Garlic walked with me to Mammy's room at the top of the stairs. He opened the door of what I remembered to be Other's room and said, simply, "It's hua's now." For a moment I thought he meant it was hers because she had died in it, or hers because she was laid out in it. As my eyes adjusted to the vanishing afternoon light, in the gloom of closed drapes, as Garlic closed the door between us, leaving me in and him out, I saw the gingham curtains, homespun upholstery, and rag rugs. I saw the few gewgaws and the many small labors: a quilt in the middle of being pieced together, a gown half-made, another rag rug on its way, and I knew Mammy lived in this room.

And she had died in it and would now be laid out in it.

Garlic closed the door and left me alone with her body. I crawled up in the bed and got closer than she would have let me get; closer than she ever let me get. I undressed her and put her into a clean white nightgown. Her huge belly, the white hair between. I looked at her belly and wondered how I had gotten into it and how I'd gotten out of it. I wondered if I had felt strangled inside. I wondered if her love of bigness, the pleasure she took in being immense, had anything to do with a love of carrying me. I hoped that it did.

I wanted to yowl. But my mouth didn't open.

After what seemed like a long while, after it seemed I could never get up from that place, it seemed like I had to get out right then. Get out or be pulled into the grave. Like the angel of death had come and might confuse us. I arose from her bed and smoothed away my presence with my hands.

Across the room from the bed, facing the window, was a high-back chair. She had seen the avenue of trees leading up to Cotton Farm from that window. I slumped into the chair and watched the road as Mammy had watched. Only I didn't know who I was watching for.

I was just there a little while before I could no longer bear the silence or the pain; I willed myself to doze. I don't believe I had been out for two minutes when the door opened.

Other didn't see me. The chairback hid me. I couldn't see her either. But I heard. First she sniffled and cried. Then she whined. She lay her head on Mammy's chest and told Mammy her troubles, like Mammy cared. Like she was telling her to fetch a shawl. She didn't see me at all. Not Other.

Maybe I slumped down low in the chair because I knew she would come. Maybe I sought to hide myself so she might be revealed. Everyone at Twelve Slaves Strong as Trees knew the story of how Other threw herself and some kind of vase at Dreamy Gentleman and of how R. heard it because he was lying down on a couch unseen. It was the one story he told me about her. And I told it to the community. Strange how on the pillow you get them to tell you—not the things you want to hear, but the things that may kill you. It was on the pillow he told me his soldiering tales.

I cleared my throat, paused a moment before rising—she could wait to see who had heard—then I rose. I stand a good three or four inches taller than she does. But her waist is smaller. Mammy used to tell me that. There are things of mine that she has taken. I could not let this hour, this visit be one of them.

She was scared, and for the first time in my life I saw her scared without her angry.

I knew if I said *boo,* she'd run out the room.

So I said, "Boo."

Or I said, "My mother and I want to be alone, ma'am. Captain R. sends his condolences, sho do. He sent some fruit for you. Sent some for me and all the folks here too."

Other ran out the room, crying.

I stepped to the door, calling softly, "Ma'am? What must I do to comfort you?"

23

*N*owadays, Miss Priss and her mother, Garlic's family, live in the old overseer's house. The house where Lady caught some fever, smallpox or scarlet, and died. Someone has ludicrously trained rosebushes to grow up the side of this slap-dash wooden structure. Most nights Garlic sleeps in Planter's old room and leaves his bed in the overseer's house empty. He's put my bags in the trellised shack; I'm to sleep in his empty bed. Before I came down from the old house, I took a bottle from Other's dining room sideboard. I hope no one misses it tonight. I help myself to a long swig.

I walk out on the porch, hoping it will help me catch my breath. There's no gas to illuminate the dark out here, only oil lamps and bee's-wax flame. It makes for a different color of night. The stars are brighter. It's hard to see to write.

There are so many things of Other's I have wanted. Things, then people. People more than things—but nothing she has ever had, no emerald, not R., have I ever wanted as much as I wanted her love for Mammy. As the sun sets, it don't hurt near as much that Mammy didn't love me as it hurts that I didn't love Mammy.

Once upon a time I loved my mother. But that love was frail and untended; I let that love die. No, it wasn't like that, like a plant in a pot deprived of water. Truth is

that love got some sort of sickness that moved so quick
and there was no doctor to tend the patient and my love
just died. I had no idea in the world how to stop that
death from coming once it started, and started coming on
quick. It was like the smallpox moving through the
house, leaving scars and death, and you're scared to see it
coming. And you never forget it came. Just like the first
time you see a dead body, you know one day death's coming for you too. The first time you stop loving somebody,
you learn all love ends. And loving somebody is just the
graceful practice of patience before the love dies.

I know exactly where my love for Mammy is buried.
Like an unembalmed beast left decaying in the yard of
my mind, it stinks the place right up to high heaven. Is
there a low heaven? Can I drift there and stay close to
her?

It hurts not to love her. And it hurt more when I didn't
—I still don't—believe she ever loved me. I close my
eyes after writing that, after making that witness, and I
wince in a breath. God damn her soul! And it's less a
curse than a fear. What do God do with folk who won't
see the beauty He put in all creation? What do He do
when He tired of hearing the angels weeping? I know
the angels weep every time a dusky Mama is blind to the
beauty of her darky child, her ebony jewel, and hungers
only for the rosebud mouth to cling to the plum moon of
her breast.

Don't I understand why Miss Priss killed Mealy

Mouth? Don't I remember Garlic's wife with Mealy Mouth and Dreamy Gentleman's Harvard-going brat at her breast? Miss Priss lost two brothers to that woman. It's all so mixed up. I take a sip more—or is it more than a sip—from Other's brandy bottle, and my memories are like fish in a bowl swimming one way and then another, detached, insignificant, but still I turn back to look, re-member, watch, mesmerized as the memories glide past.

24

R. didn't have too many bedroom memories of Other to tell, to hold back. But sometime during the afternoon that Georgia entered the war, he felt her breath on his face, and that breath left its imprint on his eye. Other never knew, didn't guess, I was the one first spoke her name to him. To get her out of my head, I put her in his. That's not what I intended to do, but I did something, and that's what happened. I was the one told him 'bout her.

I'm trying to remember about that time and get it straight. R. had gone to the picnic barbecue at Twelve Slaves Strong as Trees, gone to do a little business, he told me. I believe now he went there to see her. Other had gone in the hopes of getting Dreamy Gentleman to ask for her hand in marriage. But that was not to be, and everybody but Other had seen it a long time coming.

Dreamy Gentleman had made up his mind to marry his cousin Mealy Mouth, a flat-chested slip of a girl who would never ask more from marriage than family. She didn't have the first idea about passion between a man and a woman, but she possessed a fiery loyalty to family, particularly to her brothers, that attracted Dreamy Gentleman profoundly. He saw luscious possibilities in that loyalty. And he saw a fine line of children springing from his loins (which he coveted and hoped he deserved), golden children that would resemble his beautiful cousin, resemble all his cousins, for they greatly resembled each other.

Dreamy Gentleman was a particular friend of Mealy Mouth's brother (not the young one Other would marry; an older brother nobody really talked about). This brother played Cupid for Mealy Mouth and Dreamy Gentleman; Dreamy Gentleman could not but be slain by Mealy Mouth's brother's golden arrow. Mealy Mouth was grateful to her brother for forming the attachment.

If Other could see how tenderly Dreamy Gentleman valued loyalty and silence and how roughly he disdained feminine hunger and passion, she would not have made the drive to Twelve Slaves Strong as Trees. She would have known that she was not and had never been a featured player in the theater of his life. No wife would be.

But she was blind to all that. Other knew only every man she knew would give his life to be the object of her desire.

There had been someone Dreamy Gentleman loved, but not someone he could marry or that any of us could talk about. Miss Priss had a brother who worked for Mealy Mouth's Mama and Papa, and that brother was dead. They never feared Miss Priss after that; after her brother whipped up dead, Miss Priss went kind of simple. She seemed to want to make it all up to the family, the family, she said, over and over again, "what had been betrayed." Mealy Mouth's family thought she was talking about them. They continued to believe Miss Priss understood that a trusted family servant (even your brother) whispering a family secret (even in passion) was peculiar treachery. Garlic, who mourned his son, knew what his daughter meant. And knowing that Miss Priss possessed a keen and labyrinthine intelligence, Garlic seemed willing to let her balance the scales. He did very little to make amends. He just was.

But Miss Priss was there both times Mealy Mouth gave birth, the time she died, and the time she almost died. Miss Priss scares me. I don't think there's anything simple about her. So later, when they were all together during the war, when I lived at Beauty's and they were living at Other's Aunt Pattypit's, and Miss Priss told me how Other "throwed herself" at Dreamy Gentleman and how R. saw, I didn't tell her different. She thought R. was *see-*

ing her for the first time that day; she thought what Other thought. But he was only *meeting* her for the first time. He saw her first in his conversation with me.

It was me who told R. about Other. Even before they met, I made him see her. I didn't want to lose him, but I wanted someone who loved her to love me more than her. I made the introduction in fear with trembling. I didn't believe anybody who knew us both could love me more, but I hoped for it, and I had to know. I didn't trust Miss Priss enough to tell her how it really was then, and I don't trust her enough now, but I remember.

I fed R. from Mammy's store of how wonderful Other was—and there is something wonderful about her and it was exactly this: she has the vitality, the vigor, and the pragmatism of a slave, and into this water you stir as much refinement as you can pour without leaving any grains of sugar at the bottom of the glass. She was a slave in a white woman's body, and that's a sweet drink of cold water. In more ways than one, she thought and didn't think I was her sister. Just like in the Bible, I played Mary to her Martha, but many days it feels that it is I who have chosen the lesser part. Truth to tell, it's the lesser part what chose me. When it comes right down to it, I am Lady's child and she is Mammy's.

My mother, Lady, lost her man, Feleepe, at fifteen. When her family refused to accept him as a suitor, he ran off to some port city and was killed in a duel. Other's mother, Mammy, lived with her man all of her life, taking no public part, giving no private corner. Lady lay with Planter only the nights that were needed to bring babies. The girls who still walk this earth with me, and the boys who lay sleeping in the graveyard. Planter slept with Mammy in pleasure all their lives. In truth of body, I was the passion fruit, and Other was the bloom of civil rape. In truth of soul, Other was raised in the humidity of desire sucking boldly at Mammy's breast, and I was raised in the cool restraint of Lady's boudoir, the place to which you retreat with dignity, a place of private sorrows and private consolations, the touch of Lady's soft hand lavished on my hapless head. So Other was a child of pleasure and I a child of cold chastity, willing to be bred.

25

Garlic dug the grave. We had our service early in the morning, Garlic, his wife, Miss Priss, and me. Just dawn. The time of day when even servants rest. Maybe. I wanted an hour she had been at rest on earth, and I couldn't find one. Only in the lazy drag of her feet, the slow trifling ramble on any one of so many errands, did she save herself just a little from work-hard-work-long exertion, a slave's exertion.

There are two cemeteries on the place. Out back of where the cabins used to be, over a mile from the house, there is a slave cemetery. A concentration of round field-stones (some still in stacks) and branches lashed together to create crude crosses mark for still blinking eyes the ter-ritory of the enslaved dead. It helps to squint. The ground is soft here, damp. Some suspect an underground spring. A blanket of wild grass and wild flowers covers this ground most of the year, protecting, concealing.

Closer to the house—you can see it from the porch—is the family burial ground: a rising mound of red earth beneath a tall, limb-spreading tree. In this mound are carved stones of pink Etowah marble. Pink stones, head and feet, red earth, green tree, sprigs, and odd blades of grass. Nothing much could grow in that shade. Nothing grows in this shade but names and dates and ghosts. A low wall of flat stones piled one on top of the other, a slave wall, hedges the ghost in, hedges the visitors out.

We buried her in the family plot.

Of course, Other wants Mammy buried beside Lady. What she doesn't know is a long time ago Lady's grave and Planter's were changed, looking toward just this day. Mammy be lying down beside Planter. He got himself in the middle, in death just like in life. Only the folk at the early service know that—Garlic, his wife, Miss Priss, and me.

Garlic spoke over the body. When Lady and Mammy

come to the place, Garlic was there. He had chaperoned their entire journey from Savannah to the grave. He brought them to this side of the piney woods where both women got knocked up so big and quick. Everybody suppose Garlic put it to Mammy; the master's valet follows the master and chooses the mistress's maid. Oh, peculiar economy! It was a way of making sure there was milk for the baby. Somebody plants a seed in the going-to-be-wet-nurse, and then you starve that child if you have to, like they starved Miss Priss's younger brother. Garlic knew what not to say and what to say so that people would say less.

He braided what he could remember of the words from the Episcopal prayer book with his own words.

"You might could say we was the whole Trinity around this place, me, Mammy, and Miss Priss." His wife frowned, but we all knew what he meant. Garlic was right. Mrs. Garlic had bearing, height, and a kind of beauty that grew with age, but she had changed nothing of significance in any of our lives. Her stature was only apparent. Mrs. Garlic always stood in a kind of second command to Mammy, a shadow echo of a greater strength. Ultimately it was Miss Priss, so insignificant-seeming, so shrill, so silly, who completed the triangle that walled Cotton Farm off from the world.

Garlic was wearing the watch that I wanted for mine. I saw the golden keys hanging from it. "I was with

Planter the night he won this place in a card game. Way back when. Ain't nobody on this place know what I know 'cept Sister—that's what I came to call her—and now she gone. What I have to say I say for her. And I say it for me, 'cause when it comes time to lay me in this ground, ain't none of ya'll be knowin' what to say.

"Planter won me in a poker game. My old master was a rich young planter from St. Simon's island. Good-looking, good-mannered, we went everywhere, Charleston, N'awlins, Washington, D.C. I been to Marse Jefferson's Monticello; you name it, I been there. I was with him when he went to Harvard. I stood in the square and got me some education while he graduated on time, not like those twins from 'round here who tumbled in and out of every college. Young Marse was something else. So much so I couldn't be nothing. I stood in the Yard and he went to the classrooms. Yeah. Now this man heah" (tapping his toe on Planter's grave) "was a different matter. He didn't know nothing. He didn't have nothing but his white skin, spirit, and work-hard. He needed me. And I needed him, 'cause I had a vision of a place I wanted to live.

"So I mixed my young master's drinks heavy and poured my hoped-to-be-master's drink light. Wasn't good luck won Planter me. It was me poisoning Young Marse's cup. Later, Young Marse offered twice the money to get me back, and I was scared. But my new master, my soon-to-be Planter, was too proud of his first slave to let me go. I played the same trick when we won this land, but Planter was in on it. And it was me who told him when it was time for us to find a wife with a good group of house Negroes. I knew Mammy. When we first came to Savannah, Mammy told me all 'bout Lady and her troubles, and I told Planter what he need to know. I wanted Mammy for this place.

"There was no architect here. There was me and what I remembered of all the great houses on great plantations I had seen. Bremo. Rattle-and-Snap. The Hermitage. Belgrove. Tudor Place. Sabine Hall. I built this place with my hands and I saw it in my mind before my hands built it. Mammy and me, we saved it from the Yankees not for them but for us. She knew. She knew this house stood proud and tall when we couldn't. Every column fluted was a monument to the slaves and the whips our bodies had received. Every slave being beat looked at the column and knew his beating would be remembered. I stole for this place and I got shot doing it. We, Mammy and me, kept this place together because it was ours. Here I raised my family. Right this morning we're burying the real mistress of the house."

Right then I cried.

Later we had the official funeral. Other cried and cried. We were a pathetic band. Dreamy Gentleman bereft of

Mealy Mouth, and Other absolutely confused, confused as to why R. wasn't there. She believed it to have something to do with Beauty, that "waddling woman, with the powdered face and the colored hair."

Dreamy Gentleman had come, of course, bringing his heir and his baby; bringing Other's surviving children. There was the most exquisite kind of pain in Dreamy Gentleman's eyes when he looked into Miss Priss's face. Other saw Dreamy Gentleman looking at Priss and almost hissed. Then she saw, with her memory, what he saw: a beautiful boy's face from long ago. The face of Miss Priss's brother appeared in his sister's face when she flared her nostrils in any show of arrogance or anger. For the very first time, Other saw it, and I saw her see it. Other didn't see me at all; it was as if I didn't exist.

R. couldn't come because I was there. So Other looked down the road for him, harder than she had ever looked for Dreamy Gentleman. And she had looked hard down that road when the war was over and nobody knew who was coming home alive and with what body parts.

Dreamy Gentleman read properly from the Book of Common Prayer and gave a little talk about how we were laying to rest the last of a vanished species and culture—the loyal old servant who, Christ-like, sacrificed herself for others. He believed every word. He believed my mother to be an unselfish woman. He believed her to be a loving beast of burden without sex or resentment. He knew nothing of her at all.

And Other knew only bits more. Now, as I think back on what I saw of her at the grave, I am struck by the truth of her grief. I wonder what she would feel now if she knew, if I told her, if she ever come to understand that Mammy used her, used her to torment white men. Other was Mammy's revenge on a world of white men who would not marry her dark self and who had not loved her Lady. Did Other see how she had been weaned to pick up hearts and trained to dash them down, both with casual ease? Who convinced her to conquer? Had Mammy ever told Other the truth about Dreamy Gentleman? No. Watching Other stand by the grave, I knew for sure that Mammy had stopped wearing the mask and the mask had worn her. By the time we were born, choosing between Other and me was like choosing between paper dolls, and Other had the prettier clothes.

When the service was over, Other was awarded pride of place at the head of the line of mourners. I was to follow right behind. She marched straight ahead to the house, allowing the wind to carry her words back to me. "You should be ashamed of neglecting Mammy."

I went back in the house, sneaked into Lady's room, crawled into our bed, and cried.

26

In the afternoon, Other and Dreamy Gentleman went out driving in her carriage. When the driver come back, he say he took them over to where the house we called Twelve Slaves Strong as Trees once stood. I have forgotten their name for it. What I remember is this: there were twelve columns across the front of that slave-built house. They stood for the original twelve dark men who cleared the land. And the lines, the flutes, on those columns stood for the stripes on those slaves' backs. They didn't know any of that, but we did. The last sermon I heard my preacher in Atlanta preach, he said, "We don't need any new members; we need disciples!" Twelve slaves, twelve columns, twelve disciples. Twelve memories. The driver overheard Other say to Dreamy Gentleman she's going to build that house back up again, for him, in remembrance of what had been.

The driver say, "Dey ack jes lak brutha 'n sista now, not lak how she usta ack." There's a new understanding between them, and I'm not the only one to see it.

I take my rest in the overseer's house. Miss Priss watches Dreamy Gentleman's children. Lord have mercy! Other's son and daughter keep quietly to themselves. For the boy, born after his father died, every funeral is his father's funeral. For the girl, so young when her father was killed riding out with the Klan, every funeral is her father's funeral. And though their fathers were different men, this grief, more than their mother's blood, has become the bond between them.

Soon they will all be deeply asleep, sleep they need, asleep for the whole long night. After all this sorrow, God knows they need the comfort of Garlic's soup. And if God doesn't know, Garlic knows. And I need the house to grieve.

27

*W*e were sitting together at the kitchen table, me, Garlic, Mrs. Garlic, and Miss Priss. The rest of them had gone to sleep, won't wake till morning. Was Mrs. Garlic's kitchen now. Mammy's cap and Mammy's apron had been removed, and were already washed, folded, and put away; she had been sick a spell. Eating cornbread straight out of a skillet, drinking coffee from cracked cups. These events had never occurred in Mammy's kitchen. Chitlins on the stove were stinking up the place. If Mammy had ever wanted to eat chitlins, she would have cooked them out in the cabins. Freedom had a flavor, and we were tasting it. I breathed in the pungent aroma of change.

I had to ask. Everything was different, so maybe now

was my chance. "Tell me about those little boys buried out there under the tree? Lady's boys."

"What dey der da tell?" asked Mrs. Garlic, handing me a steaming bowl of pig entrails.

"You tell me," I said, hands still limp in my lap. My hunger for knowledge was sharper than my hunger for midnight food. I looked—forlornly, I hope—into Mrs. Garlic's eyes.

Miss Priss's arm shot out; she grabbed the first bowl for herself. Between noisy chomps she declared, "You should a figured it out already."

I am still hungry. I wanted to slap Miss Priss. Slap her hard. But I didn't do it. It always been this way with me. I'll call another girl "bitch" before you blink, but I don't like to hit a woman. I guess it always felt like too much of a man to do it. Strange enough. Strength always seemed to rob the girl out of me, so I always take care to keep it hid. I let my eyelids rest heavily upon my eyes and close.

Garlic's chomping down on his bowl of tripe. "Yah shouda' akse me."

"Would you tell me?"

"I knows all about it."

Garlic was playing with me like a cat batting at cobwebs, and I was dissolving and falling to the ground with each bat. I hate to be denied. I don't ask for things I can't have. I couldn't say more. But I was racing 'round the furniture in my mind, trying to find a chair to sit on. Why do I always think of it just that way? Is thinking truly like house cleaning? Finally I stumbled into an observation of Beauty's: "It's like a bad taste in your mouth to be the only person who knows something, something good or something bad. Being the only one is bitter. Being one of two is sweet." "I'll keep your secret with you," I offered.

Garlic say nothing.

I rose as if to walk away. I said, "It's like starting to disappear at your beginning end. Ain't it?"

"What?"

"Forgetting. If I forget what happened to me in Charleston and you don't know it to remind me, it's gone. A year of my life gone like termites eating out the middle of a wood board, vanished into a mouth and flown away. Gone with the wind."

"When ebrybody knowed what happened and why is dead."

"You remember who I used to be. I got nobody in 'lanta to do that for me."

"Now you admittin' that it you what needs me. I'm surrounded with memory." Garlic pulled me by the arm into his life, pushing me into a closer chair.

"We've spent enough time in this kitchen," said Mrs. Garlic. Wife and daughter got up and left us alone.

28

I've always been afraid of Garlic. He never treated me warm-like. I remember seeing him toss other children on the place—black and white—into the air to catch in his powerful arms. I remember seeing him sneak lumps of sugar to Jeems when he was about the place, but not to me.

Garlic poured a lot of milk in a cup, into which he stirred sugar, then a splash or two of coffee. Something in the way he slurped disturbed me. His lower lip poked so far out, it grabbed at the cup as if it were a third thumb. "How many time I sit in dis kitchen with huah when all de house sleep?"

"How many times?"

"You think you smart?"

"I hope I am."

"Dat's da trufe. When we brought ya Mama to de house, it was huah and me late nights in dis kitchen. First you was coming, I hoped you were my baby. But then you came with what dey called peridot green eyes. Pallas cried when she saw you wrapped in the little blanket. You were so clear white till your color came in. As little of it as you got."

He laughed. I had never heard Garlic laugh before. It was a rolling, gutbucket cough of a laugh, like the clacking together of bones in a jar.

"What was it like when you first came here?"

"I didin know nothin' but slavery times. I was born in this here country. All I could see to lifting me up was pulling real close to a powerful man and teasing him into thinking my thoughts was his own. Your daddy was the man I found. Together we found Pallas. That was your mother's name. She had already found Lady. Now Pallas, she had it kinda easy, but it's easy what will corrupt you. Lady was cut from a strange cloth, and I guess it was Pallas what cut her."

Pallas. My mother's name is Pallas. Not Mammy. Pallas.

As he told the story, Lady was fifteen years old, a heart-heavy virgin, when they came upon her. "A heart-broke child, something just like her first girl is now." Other, he was talking about. "It was a stroke of good luck that boy bein' kilt."

"Good luck?"

"Feleepe, dyin'. Lady loved her some Feleepe, and Mammy sho did love Lady. But Feleepe had money, and slaves of hid own, and he want to live right up dere in Savannah. If Lady a married him, Pallas a been a slave. When he got kilt, Pallas was sorry for Lady, but she saw her own good chance. If Lady married a man on a lonely place, a man with no people, Pallas could run the place, and she'd be free, free as she was going to be. And I knew me a man just like that."

Mammy put the idea of the convent in one of Lady's

ears and the idea of Planter in the other. Then she took her chance. Lady was leaning toward the convent. But her Daddy, he hated the Catholic Church more than he hated Catholics, and Planter was one. He couldn't bear to see his little gal given over to the Catholics. So she married Irish Planter, and if she didn't care, it was because Pallas kept feeding her something by the spoonful that didn't make your pain go away but made you stop caring that you hurt.

"I rode wid 'em up country. It was me and Mammy up front with Planter and Lady behind."

On the honeymoon, Planter came to the room and found Lady knocked out, completely drunk, sleeping in Mammy's arms. "I wa' standin' right outside the door in case things didn't go right," Garlic told me. He said, "Mammy say to Marse, 'Do yah bidness and git out.'" He didn't see what happened, and the room was quiet. Later, Mammy told him. She washed Lady's body and carried her back to her bed after she, Mammy, change the sheets. Then Mammy went to Planter in his room and gave him what he wanted in his bed. She gave it so good, he never complained. Mammy say Lady came to think of her baby as an immaculate conception like the priests in Savannah gabbled about. Between them, they called Lady "Virgin Mary." She like to pray, and she got her babies without ever knowing a man.

That's all I can write down now.

29

The bottle I took from the sideboard is almost empty. If I stay here much longer, I'll need another one. I've got to write this down. But I don't want to.

"What did she say when she found out they sold me?"

"She didin know."

"She didin know." Those three words mean more to me than "I love you." And they just as hard to believe. Garlic would lie for Mammy. Love. Ignorance. Lying. How you supposed to know anything? God? Springs of faith? Weed patches of blindness with pretty little dandelions growing in them? I like to think, I would like to think, she didn't know. I see into this thing too deeply. Maybe she sent me away, for me. Once I was gone, she had to forget me, or she, Pallas, would a died of pain. I know all about it. Didn't I do the same? Forget or die of pain. Die of pain while I learned to forget?

Miss Priss came back to the kitchen for her cup of coffee. Miss Priss looked at me hard. She asked if she could read my palm.

"What do you see?" There's something sly and intelligent about Miss Priss, but the whites don't see it.

"Not'ing, I see not'ing."

"Why you shivering?"

"It gives me the heebie-jeebies to stand out in that

graveyard. It's strange, all those little boys buried right next to your Mama."

"Why strange?"

Garlic tried to silence Miss Priss with a look, but she kept carrying forward, and he just banged out of the room, taking a cup of coffee out to his wife in the parlor. Miss Priss let her voice drop real low, low in pitch and low in loudness. She kind of hissed into my ear. "Your Mama killed those boys soon as they were born."

"Why would she do that?"

"What would we a done with a sober white man on this place?"

30

Me gone to sleep and got up again. The house, Garlic's house, is cold, silent, dark. It feels so different to know this was Garlic's dream and not Planter's. Not my father's.

Garlic pulled the string, and Planter danced like a bandy-legged Irish marionette. Everything but the horseback riding. That was his. There was always something African about Planter, and Garlic was it. Even Planter's love of the land had something African in it. Black people are ancestor worshippers. And they have the sense of sacred places. Me heard the stories. My heart is still crick-crack-breaking. There's a bright bitter feeling snaking down my chest. I don't feel my heart beat, but I want to.

My forehead sweats hot beads, my hands sweat cold. My nose is beige and my mother's black. I look at my fingers and sometimes I think the tips of them are purple. I look at my face and see a faint redness on the cheeks, as if a scarlet butterfly landed on my face while I was sleeping and left its rouging flying-dust.

Now what has Garlic told me? That he helped Planter win him in a card game by poisoning his old master, Planter's opponent. That he chose to work for Planter because Planter was an impotent man. Oh, God! What God do I now imagine in heaven? Where are his hair of gold and eyes of blue? My Daddy's eyes. The only God I knew built Cotton Farm, ran the slaves on this place. Now that ain't Planter. Ain't Daddy. Now what? Now Planter was a man without position or land who Garlic manipulated with his black hands into winning our land from another white man in a card game. Garlic the poisoner. I would laugh if it were not so sad. I would laugh if every laugh didn't jostle loose bitter burps of knowing, leaving vinegar vapor on my tongue, the only vestige of the illusion of my father's power.

31

I am leaving here today. The place where I was born. I wish I had not come back. The three little graves, the boys' graves, the heirs' graves. It's like this—Mama kill those children? Or not. Ain't sure which way I want it to be. I think I don't want her to have done it. And then I feel, if she did it, I know for sure she loved me. Loved me enough to kill. And it hard for someone who ain't a killer to kill.

Miss Priss told me long time ago of how Other and Mealy Mouth killed the soldier. Knifed him to death, on the steps, with his own sword. They pretended like they hadn't. But dark eyes see everything on a place like this. Or do they see nothing? I've seen nothing. I know how every inch of this place smells, and you can't change a place without changing its smell. I kinda loved her for killing that soldier. All of them did. They said he needed killing and couldn't be no black to do it, so they was glad Other did it. Mama rested easier with the smell of murder gone from the place. That's how we all knew Other wasn't a natural-born killer. And Mama and Garlic weren't neither, for the smell of killer was gone from the place when the soldier died.

How happy can I be? Must I cry? I believe I must go, and keep going. There is nothing left for me here. I've

had no word from R.; she's had two formal, kind mis-
sives. What will I find back in Atlanta upon my return?
An abandoned house? A place to work at Beauty's?
What?

Garlic will make arrangements for me to leave. It will
be easier for them when I am gone. And it will be easier
for me.

32

*J*eems rode me back to Atlanta behind his horse, Han-
nibal. It's strange to think of Jeems driving his own horse
and not one belong to the Twins or to their place. It's
stranger than the Twins being dead. We all knew one day
they would die, but no one knew one day Jeems would
drive his own horse. Jeems is a good-looking man. I wonder I ain't seen it before. I guess it's what a fine-looking
man he's become. I wonder what he would have been if
the Twins had survived the war. Something less.

He's built a house for himself and a church for the
community, he tells me while we're riding, but did I see
he's not settled? Did he seem less each time he swung
down from the horse? And don't he look fine with reins
in his hand? A hammer give not quite the same effect.
But he's a farmer during the week and a preacher on

Sunday. He milks his cow every day, and don't ride enough.

He told me all this and I laughed and tried not to laugh too hard. Ever since I heard Garlic's laugh, I've been laughing too much, off and on, all the time, like crying. Jeems, he watched me laugh.

"Ever think on getting married, gal?"

"You asking me?"

"Why should I akse you?"

I laughed again. There was no reason he would ask me. I knew and he knew I knew it. So he surprised me when he said, "Maybe I'm aksing you." I didn't laugh. The words jangled in my head like pennies in a jar—not enough to buy something with but enough for the sound to strangle thought. Nobody ever put that question to me. And I didn't expect to ever hear it on a ride down from the country to the city. From a man I ain't kissed. I'm greedy for a second serving of those words. I want a dessert of those words, a soup, a salad. I wanted to salt those words and snap them in like peanuts. But Jeems is a friend back to sugar-tit days.

"Don't ask me."

"I'm asking you. Will you marry me?"

"I'm not the marrying kind."

"You not or he ain't?"

"I ain't. My Mama never married. We don't marry."

"Too bad," Jeems said and he clucked the horse on.

We walked on down the road. "How's Miss Kareen?"

"Miss...?"

"Kareen."

"She's in a convent."

"I know that. In Charleston. How she be?"

"Why you ask 'bout her?"

"She was the one we really liked."

The words fall on me hard, like a blow—a smack across the face, a slap on my rumpass, leaving the bright red blood tattoo of a hand. "We—you mean the Twins?"

I thought it was Other they sniffed after. I thought the homefolks thought Kareen's moaning over B. was some kind of too much sorry-for-yourself play-acting.

"We all loved Sugarbaby. B. was fixin' fo to marry hua. Woulda, 'cept for Gettysburg. S. was sweet on yo' sister."

"I don't have a sister." I didn't get the words out to say S. nor any other Southern gentleman would marry a nigger, when Jeems interrupts with one sly, snarled word: "Yeah."

I was ashamed for Mama and ashamed for not knowing he knew. I knew who he meant. And I knew he knew I knew. Why do I get stuck in these little circles?

Mammy didn't marry; I suspect I won't either. He asked me if I had a reason. And I just stared at him, letting him take the answer to be no. But it's like this. Long ago. Long ago. How long ago? I don't even know. I stopped letting myself want anything I could not have.

Hours later Jeems pulled the carriage up in front of my house and I got out.

33

R. wanted to know who the boy was who had brought me back from Cotton Farm. I wanted to wince when he spoke "boy," but I answered, "Jeems," and gave him my smile. For the first time, the first time ever, I'm wondering what it was he did remember about before Emancipation. "You remember the Twins Other was sweet on?"

"Those big red-haired boys?"

"Them."

He nodded, but there was an unspoken question hiding in his smile.

"Jeems was their tenth birthday present. He was ten too."

"The Twins are dead now."

"Yeah, they are."

"Gettysburg."

"Gettysburg."

Already R. had lost interest. He wasn't interested in slaves. I tried another smile, but my mouth sort of stuck to my teeth, and all I made was something that looked like snaggles peeking through half a moon. My face was changing. I wondered if he could see it yet. I smiled the half-broken smile that conceals. I achieved a fraction more. The edges of my lips were heavy, and I could feel the inside of my lips sticking to my teeth. Always, when I'm awkward or clumsy, I'm grateful for beauty which causes men not to notice my other imperfections.

I wanted to ask R. if he was grateful for my beauty, but I did not. Questions like that can only be written here. They can't breathe. Is he ever grateful for anything I do?

I told him I was tired, and he told me to be down in time for the evening meal. I told him dust was with me still. Dust of death and dust of road. I needed sleep, day sleep now, and water. I blinked, and then I wanted to cry with no cause.

He said, "Be down in time for supper. A Congressman is coming to dine."

At noon the young maid brought dinner up to my room: cold fried chicken and a glass of wine. She is an olive-skinned, straight-haired girl, a slim-as-a-beanpole beauty, heavy on her feet, but there is a lot of Indian in her nigger. She closed the door behind her when she entered. Just then she appeared a breathless, hipless, and unsexed creature. The drumming of her feet as she crossed my room, placing the tray or unpacking my bag or storing clothes away in the chifforobe, lulled me to sleep. I fell asleep and dreamed of Jeems.

It was a very bad dream. I dug up the grave of the last of the dead baby boys. The one born the year I went away. I dug into his grave, opened the coffin, and Jeems popped out, live, like a jack-in-the-box. He had a hundred white teeth. There were too many teeth, but they were so pretty, like pearls bright shining, and I was glad he had so many yet repulsed at the same time. I wanted him to stop grinning so he would still have the teeth but I wouldn't see them.

But he wouldn't stop grinning, and I couldn't get the lid of the coffin back on. I woke up with sweat and tears running down my face. I just had time to dress.

34

I'll be late down to supper now. But R. say the Congressman will be later. I hope Mrs. Dred larded the turkey enough so the meat won't be dry with long cooking. Of all our peculiar customs, I find it strange that we denizens of the Southland don't have a taste for cool food —even in August. I told her to wrap the turkey in bacon before cooking, but she knows I don't like to serve the turkey with the bacon on it, so I suspect the bacon is someone's dinner and not on the turkey at all, and I can't be angry. Everybody needs to eat.

R. came into the room and led me to the bed. He lay me down upon it. And undressed me as if I was a child. He sat down beside me. He kissed my forehead and my lips. Ran his hand across my belly. His hand just hovered over the curly dark separating my thighs. When he looked at me this way, I knew he wouldn't love me. Wouldn't touch me. Wouldn't take me.

I still stir his mind, but I can no longer for sure stir his body. He is still beautiful. Men seem to start glowing with years. I wonder if they shine with the invisible candles that light up good leather when it ages. He wears his wealth on his face. Life has carved a leanness into the bones of my man that the years of plenty and the years of excess, drink and food, do not blight—completely.

Light in August. I used to be scared I would have a baby. Now I am scared I will not. My waist is narrow as a virgin's, and my stomach is babyless flat, my breast babyless high. I like to think I wear my years lightly. Virgins go dry and age quickly into brittle spinsters. Women who are touched by many different men become shopworn angels. You can see the smudges of bourbon breath mottling their eyes. Mothers grow flaccid, rich in baby love, each baby taking some of the mother's beauty as if the baby knows it needs to protect its babyself by making Mama less kiss-daddy pretty. Each baby knows the baby to come takes something away from the baby in arms, so little Jenny and little Carrie cry in the night just when

Daddy's rising. They gray Mama's hair and suck the full-ness out of her breast. Filling her heart with such love, she don't need to look in the mirror to see who she is. I learned all that at Beauty's. What the babies take away, the girls paint back on.

Me, I'm looking in the mirror, still. The mirror on the wall and the mirror in his eyes. I see Beauty grow blowsy; I see Other grow wider with the laying of three men and the birthing of three babies. Me — I've only had one man and no babies, and so my skin is not etched like marble with the pale wiggling seams where life stretched forth to cover life — but I am greedy for weight, the weight of life growing within me, the relief the old cow knows when she delivers in July and is light in August.

"Do you ever think about marrying me?" he asks.

"No."

"I'm thinking about marrying you."

I sit up on the bed. I don't look at him. It's time to get my dress on. I smell dinner ready in the kitchen. I won-der if Cook did lard the turkey. R. kisses me again on the forehead. For the first time in a long time, I wonder how much I remind him of Other and how much in his eyes I resemble their child. He outlines the curve of my eye-brow, and I know he is thinking of them.

I had to get this down. But now I have to dress. I will put on the red gown and the large gold hoops in my ears. I had intended to choose a more subdued dress, but I feel, after R.'s declaration, it will be amusing to play with his notion of who I am and watch him squirm. He's playing with me. I will not play in the shadow of Other.

35

The Congressman was colored. And I could not have been more charmed. I wish I could have changed gowns. Unfortunately, all he did was find fault with me, too many faults for a different dress to have helped.

There were three of us at table. Instead of placing our guest between us, R. sat me in the middle as a kind of no man's land. Each man sat at a head of the table.

I wished from the moment I walked in that I hadn't worn my hoops. Under the Congressman's gaze the hoops felt niggerish and the deepness of the cut of the bosom of my gown seemed sluttish.

But R. seemed pleased. He expected the Congressman to admire me, so all he saw was admiration.

The dinner began slowly. There was some kind of soup, a hot soup served in handled cold creamed soup bowls that made me cringe, and the turkey was dry. We had chess pie for dessert, a recipe that come over from Tennessee, like pecan pie without the pecans. It was an after-the-war food, elegant in its unadorned poverty. The

Congressman smiled at his first crispy-sweet bite.

R. caught this, and laughed. "You don't believe me. Cindy is not your ordinary lady—she's been on the Grand Tour."

"My goodness." For the first time the Congressman was impressed.

"You and Mrs. Hemmings?"

"Mrs. Hemmings?"

"Mrs. Hemmings who Jefferson took to Paris."

R. and the Congressman begin to share a laugh at my expense. To veer back to politeness the Congressman directed another question to me.

"What ship did you cross over on?"

"The *Baltic*."

"How funny, how very funny."

Now the Congressman was laughing anew, and I was laughing too. We *knew* about the *Baltic*. Only R. was still laughing at the old, cold joke, embedded like an insect in amber, that the slave Hemmings' stay in Paris had been a Grand Tour. And while we free Negroes were laughing at the strangeness of transformations, I was wondering what Lady would think of my table.

Later, when I poured them coffee and they were enjoying their cigars, before their business began in earnest and I would retire, the Congressman asked R. if he was following the career of "my friend Francis L. Cardozo. You might be useful collaborators."

"The state treasurer?" responded R.

"Exactly."

"I know the name."

"He was educated in Glasgow and in London. He was a minister in New Haven. Since the war he's been the principal of a school for blacks in Charleston. Next time you're in Charleston, you should see him."

R. shrugged. His cigar had gone out. He lit it again.

"It would be interesting to meet with him in Washington. Or bring him to see us in Atlanta."

R. changed the subject. If he was interested in the South's new colored leaders, he wasn't interested in them in his beloved old seaside town. He might eat with them in Atlanta or Washington, but he would never eat with them in Charleston.

I wonder what this means for me?

And I wondered if the Congressman had raised Cardozo's name at just that time, the moment I was pouring, to raise just that question in my mind.

36

I crossed the Atlantic Ocean on a ship called the *Baltic*. The crossing took seventeen days. My hate of seawater did not emerge until I was upon it for at least three or four. It popped up the way one of the sailors said that icebergs do. Out of the fish-rich darkness emerges this white, killing thing. Pointing straight up to the sky. A ship is like a cotton farm. Everyone has his place. There are the officers and the sailors. From the officers' uniforms dangle brass buttons that sparkle like stars against the blue, the way soldiers' buttons do.

When I first saw R. in his soldier's uniform, I wondered who he had got it off, what dead boy or man. Whose skin did he inherit? Or is my skin the only skin that has been inherited in this—dare I say it—family?

It was during the burning of Atlanta; it was late in the war.

Or did he just buy that uniform in a store? I know you don't buy them in a store. Did he have it made up, in preparation? When did he know, when did he become a soldier in the South? A Confederate officer willing to die, to keep me—different from the sailors on the ship. The sailors who live in the hole and have more work and less water and no brass buttons, the difference between them and me—words on paper. I had the softer labor.

Words on paper, a bill of sale written out at the slave market in Charleston, a name and a price. The girls who sell themselves at Beauty's are saved the pain of words on paper; their prices disappear, spoken and forgotten in the air. The most free slaves are the ones who cannot read or write.

Later, I read about the *Baltic*. It carried supplies for the relief of Fort Sumter. I guess the Congressman had read about it too. Read and remembered.

37

*A*tlanta looks small this morning when I went go out walking. Everything's so new. I smell the creosote in the train smoke and I remember wanting to go places, but I don't want anything now. Except to sit on the platform of the Atlanta train station and watch the folks coming and going, kissing and leaving.

Mama's dead, and I'm feeling old. I'm up next. It's my turn to die. R. wants to move to Charleston. He wants to begin again. His daughter is dead. Every day all day so many events—but these two deaths are the center around which the rest of both our lives revolve. One was inevitable, the other a miracle. If Precious had lived, R. would never have thought of marrying me.

When his father was living, he felt the spit of paternal hypocrisy falling down on his city, on Charleston, like rain. He grew leery of the hypocrisy of the old place, the citizens who loved the oldness of their town but denounced with silence the vigorous sinners who had built it. They were an old family, and R. was descended from the best of the original line of bold sinners. He had not changed but he kept hoping the town would, that it would reach back beyond its proper present and allow him place. Somehow, with his father's death, R. seemed to think all his critics had vanished. All his longing glances were backward. Well, let him go to Charleston and see what he finds.

38

No sooner was R. out my door than I sent a message 'round to Jeems, asking him to come by the house to take some cakes back to Garlic. Then I ransacked my cookbooks for Excellency cake or Bonaparte cake or Presidential cake—something that would taste just like who I now knew Garlic to be, Garlic's position. Finding nothing equal to my new understanding of the man, I adapted a cake, exchanging bourbon and adding walnuts —a little bow to his hard outside and strength. I covered my confection with a golden brown maple-flavored icing and called it Empire cake. Cook was taking more golden layers out of the oven when the messenger returned, note in hand, having looked all over for Jeems. Figuring Jeems must a set off for home, he gave up.

I beat butter for the icing all afternoon long, it seemed. One of my tears slipped into the butter and I beat it in. The salt of the tear was a perfect foil to the sweetness of the butter. I smiled to think of how I had achieved perfection of the flavor.

When had R. grown old? When did he stop being Other's husband? How will I know? How will I let myself know? When did I start loving R.? Had it stopped? Could it stop? Had I ever really loved him, or had I just wanted what was hers? Was he mine before he was hers? Was it me he saw when he first saw her walking down the steps of Twelve Slaves Strong as Trees? We had been lovers for over a year then. When did I first hear that he had met her? I remember all the pages I had covered with my name changed to end with his. All the fake letters I signed Mrs. R— B—, never thinking one day my name might change. Now, with a tear of a blue velvet riding habit, muddied, bloodied, never to be cleaned, all is possible. Was no more wanted than this extraordinary cake drawing ants?

39

I wonder if Jeems can read. I've decided to write him a letter. It's going to say:

Dear Jeems,
    Thank you for riding me to town. It's nice to remember old friends.

I was wondering how to close the letter when Jeems knocked right on the front door. I must have looked surprised. "This here's yo' front do', ain't it? This ain't Cap'n B house, is it?"

"It's my house."

I had never before had colored company of *my own* in the front room; now Jeems sat on my sofa visiting *me*. For a moment I stopped to wonder what Jeems would think, seeing me surrounded by such wealth. Then I remembered myself. We had exchanged our earliest confidences in silk-wallpapered halls and richly furnished corners. We had both dusted and mopped and washed too many fine things, too much Limoge, too much Wedgwood, too many times, to retain awe. The former field slaves will have different relations to wealth (the wealth they see and the wealth they attain) than we, who, like Jeems and me, worked in the house. Familiarity, even with things, breeds contempt.

"Our Congressman from Alabama came for dinner the other night."

"Sure like to meet him. Wonder if he knows Smalls."

"Smalls?"

"The colored Congressman who seized *Planter* in '62. Sailed the ship right over to the Union Army."

"How do you know that?"

"I was *in* the Confederate Army. I was all tore up when it happened." For a fleeting moment Jeems let his face-o-woe mask distort his features. But it just didn't fit anymore. It popped off; he was laughing. "Cried crocodile tears."

"I'm sure you did. And now?"

"And now I'm on my way to Tennessee."

"Tennessee?"

"I'm no farmer."

"They have something more than farms in Tennessee?"

"Horses."

"Ain't that Virginia, or Kentucky?"

"Tennessee. I've got some family living on a plantation just outside of Nashville. Belle Meade. They breed fine horses there. They could use a man like me."

Pieces of our world were just spinning off. Ever since Emancipation. Big and little pieces. Before we never went anywhere.

"Back when you were a young gal, you remember me from then?"

"I was never young."

"Little, then."

"Of course."

"When I was little, I got whipped for you."

"I don't remember that."

"You didn't get whipped."

"How I get you in trouble?"

"Trouble was there; you didn't get me in it. I let you

ride my horse. You were ten or eleven. I was thirteen or fourteen. Planter came down and saw you legs spread around that animal, saw it was my horse you was on, and whipped up some pain on me."

"I remember riding. You never looked at me after that."

"I'd like to take you riding again."

"I'd like that too."

"Would he mind it? Would it matter if he did?"

"No and yes."

"No and yes?"

"He would mind ... if he bothered to notice."

"But if a white man ..."

"Or some white man might mind for him. Someone who thinks Cap'n still owns you."

And it be worse than a beating Jeems would catch. They're hanging black men all through the trees. Strange fruit grow in the Southern night. It's the boil on the body of Reconstruction, whites killing blacks. They didn't kill us as often, leastways not directly, when they owned us. All I will remember about Jeems is he caught a beating. There have been so many more pictures of Jeems in my head. Off to the side of those tall, red, laughing boys (who did the Grand Tour not of Europe but of the Southern universities), a lithe, taller man, observant, graceful Jeems. So many pictures, if in most, he, like me, was way off to the side in my mind's memory. But all those memory pictures started vanishing with a blow to my head, a blow of knowledge. He'd caught a beating for me, and I had never even known.

He asked me how I was keeping. He told me he was sad for me about my Mama. His pity was too much. I told him not to be. I wanted to be asking him not to leave if he pitied me so much, but my old habit of not asking for what I won't get is strong. I was angry he was leaving, and jealous that he could imagine escaping the world we knew. I shook my head and told him the truth — because I thought it would hurt him. I told him I hadn't known my mother well and she didn't know me.

I had intended to silence him, but instead my candor loosened his mouth. He too had a tale to tell about mothers, much to my surprise.

"I never knew, I don't know who my Mama is. They bought me when I was a baby. Some idea Miz had to raise me with the Twins, so I could be their slave but not have 'niggerish' ways. Almost everything best about me is niggerish ways. But that's my defiance, and my defiance is pure Miz. I'm pure African and I got a mulatto mind. That's me. Listen here, gal. Think on this. I 'member Miz always said to the boys she didn't want them marryin' Lady's daughters, not any of 'em. She said, 'You can't divide Lady from Mammy.' Nobody knew what she mean, but I say, if it's true you can't divide Mammy from Lady, maybe you can't divide Lady from Mammy."

Now what that supposed to mean? I wanted to ride back with Jeems to Cotton Farm, to the answers those acres might provide, to a little more time with him. But he's only stopping back home before going on to Tennessee, straightaway. He's not stopping back through Atlanta, and I'm not returning home. I sent Garlic his cake in the mail.

40

$\mathcal{W}$here did I think I was going? Who did I think I was going to? I got a letter from the plantation — that's what it is really, not a cotton farm — in response to mine. Can I even remember who wrote it? Does it matter? None of them really write, so somebody said it to somebody who wrote it down. Then they send it to me. They don't want me. I'm not welcome. They say, "She still here." Other, they mean. "Mammy gone. Ain't no reason for you to come here now."

I know that; I got to laugh. Yeah. Now. Whoa. Garlic. Garlic doing what Garlic do, protect the place. I see it. If Other find me there, Other may fall in hate with the place. She may realize 'bout R. and me. May remember something about Lady and me. My slave fear falls in beside me. That old fear that should be getting old, turning brown and be easy to blow into the wind, is ever green like the earth is ever red. Garlic's scared, I'm scared, that old fear that what we love might be sold: Mamas, Daddys, children ... the place ... a dress ... anything we love.

It's an old confusion, people turning into things. When folks is gone (sold, dead, run-off), you got a corn husk doll, a walnut-shell ring, fingertips of dirt on the hem of a dress. It happened so much, maybe now things turn into people. The house, Tata — Garlic could hear it speak. All it contained of the brown lives it had eaten; it was a living thing. Garlic walks into the great hall of the house like R. pushes in between my thighs; his eyes scream, "Sugar walls, sugar walls." Everything sweats in the heat. Garlic won't permit anything that might provoke Other to sell the place. Won't put Cotton Farm at risk at all. It's his sacred place.

I come to see what I ain't seen before. Me on the place might taint it. Soon she'll come back to 'lanta, and I'll see what Garlic say then.

41

R. is involved in some kind of foreign currency exchange scheme. He came to know a good many foreign bankers during the war, when he was selling cotton on the foreign markets.

At home the pendulum seems to swing again, swinging away from the promise of real change: the change from little boys and little girls picking cotton to children reading and writing and wearing shoes and eating every day and one day getting to vote or getting to influence their father's or their brother's vote. It's like being pregnant. You are or you are not. A child has those things or does not. Conservative victories ended Congressional Reconstruction in Virginia before the state was admitted back into the Union—was it just last year? Was it 1870?

Reading or not, voting or not, these changes are small but necessary. They are the salt on the meat of our existence, eating or not, sheltered or not, living or not. Alabama, Arkansas, Florida, Mississippi—we're holding on to our votes there, even R.'s beloved South Carolina. When 1880 comes, I fear and he hopes, it will not look so very different for so very many from 1860.

But it will look different for me.

I want him to take me on a boat to Assisi or Florence, some place like that, some place I ain't seen, some place we could see together. Dublin, maybe. Dublin's good. I used to hear Planter talk about there. Or Egypt. I like it when he tells me Egyptian stories and calls me Cleopatra, except the snake bit her. Some folks say my house is a cross between Egyptian Revival and Charleston architecture. Some folks say my columns look like bundles of broomsticks. R. says they look just like bundles of papyrus reeds. I know I own three of Mr. Shakespeare's plays, *Romeo and Juliet, Cleopatra,* and *Othello.* Nurse reminded me of Mama. She didn't know who Juliet was and couldn't do nothing to protect her, really.

I asked him this morning at breakfast; he says I must wait.

I'm tired of reading and writing and cooking two meals when I don't have Cook in. I have a little business. From the money R. gives me, sometimes I make little loans to the freemen. They pay me back. I made a loan today. Other has a business. Beauty has a business. Other got men working for her; Beauty's got gals. Me, I got R., but R.'s done working. Now, he invests and sometimes it looks like he's chasing respectability the way he used to chase money, and sometimes it looks like he's chasing power.

Some of the freemen I loan money to come from Cotton Farm. Everybody say Other feeling Mammy's death hard. She doing poorly. Her beauty just about drained from her. I think that's the reason she doesn't come back to town. I look in the mirror and wonder if the same thing has happened to me and I stay blind to it. It is one of the good things about being colored — we don't show our age until all at once, all of a sudden, we need to. Then we get fat and old quick, quick enough to keep away those we need to keep away. I've heard R. talk about it. The orthodox ladies shave their heads and the yellow nigger girls get fat. Either way, only their own man wants them.

R. loves the old ways of Savannah and Charleston and N'awlins; only these cities are old enough for him now. I used to be his exotic adventure, and now it is I who is old and familiar. Other is just a reminder of the dearly departed. He takes me in his arms like a child now, and I know he can see his little girl's smile on my face. Planter's smile. I wonder if that is why he turns away from me.

42

R. brought me a ring back from Charleston. As if we could marry before they divorce. As if everyone will forget he was a war profiteer before he was a blockade buster; as if I can forget he was a Confederate soldier.

The ring sits on my finger gold and green. And I can't help liking it, because it looks like something Other would have liked. If I die and he gave the ring to her, she would wear this emerald never even knowing it had been on my finger. Some things are so pretty, you wear them even when you know where they've been. Most times, most folks, you just don't know.

I say the ring is perfect. The stone is perfect. R. says when you looking to see if you got a real jewel, you look for the flaws. I don't know what he's talking about. Sometimes he just talks.

I wonder where we would be married. In my little gray African Methodist Episcopal church, Bethel, or in his big white plain Episcopal one?

L. P. Grant gave the land for the "African church" before I was born. After the war he claimed he "never gave the lot for free negroes to worship on, but for slaves." He wanted his land back. In the end, Bethel got Grant's land and Grant's anger. He loved the little black congregation enough to give it the land, but he hated when it asserted its independence from the white Southern Methodist Church. But then again, it was prominent white citizens who pressed Grant to let Bethel keep his land.

I wonder what preacher we could ask. "I will not to the marriage of true minds admit impediments," R. said. He said and I couldn't help thinking, "Bare ruined choirs, where late the sweet birds sung." Where is that from? All these bits and pieces of "edjumacation" I have sewn together in my mind to make me a crazy quilt. I wrap it 'round me and I am not cold, but I'm shamed into shivering by the awkward ways of my own construction. All the different ways of talking English I throw together like a salad and dine greedily in my mongrel tongue.

Still, I wear the ring, and my hand sparkles when I wiggle my fingers. I lift my hand and wiggle my fingers. I follow my fingers with my eyes. I look at my pretty fingers and feel like a baby in a basket wiggling her toes, giggling to see them. I wiggle my fingers and watch. I am the actress and the audience. I am complete in my admiration of my performance. I applaud myself privately with these fingers in my bird's nest.

Sometimes you got to celebrate yourself.

Once it was only his hand that pleasured me. Those were sweet years, a time I sought to lose myself in him. It took a white-hot grown-man flame to distract me from little-girl pain. He did that for me. And I remember it.

I looked into his face tonight and it promised the face that was not there. It came to the front of my mind what I was looking for. The front of my head feels like a house, and the thoughts reside within different set places that I can rearrange like furniture, but mostly I don't. I come from a furniture-dodging tribe. We tiptoe around the pieces as they remain in place. I'm thinking that way again. Strange, the small things that make us proud.

43

We are going to Washington. The one old city I had forgotten. R. says he's taking me to walk through the halls of power, but I get gooseflesh like there's someone walking on my grave. I don't know much about Washington, but it kind of feels like walking into the belly of a beast. When I sleep tonight I hope I dream of Jonah and he looks like me.

44

If Atlanta is a city of wood, Washington is a city of brick. And it's not *all* so very old.

R.'s rented a house on 34th Street. It isn't far from the canal. The road is cobblestone and the sidewalks are red brick and the houses are real close together. They say the city is built on a swamp and you can't stay here in the summertime.

There are rich black families here.

They say the dusky Syphaxes are related to General Washington. There's a world of colored people here who were free before the war.

Other is writing him, imploring him to come back.

His maid slips her letters to my maid, who slips the letters to me.

45

I saw the President's house. It looks like a wedding cake. I wonder if I'll ever go in. I wish I could ask R. directly. We went to see a play at the Ford's Theater. A woman's dress caught fire. Some of these new dyes are so dangerous. We are staying in the Willard Hotel while the inside of our house is painted. Julia Ward Howe wrote "The Battle Hymn of the Republic" when she stayed here. She heard Union troops outside her window singing "John Brown's Body" and decided they needed something more serious. Me, I favor "John Brown's Body." What could be more serious than "moldering in the grave"? This morning we went to a little church across Lafayette Square from the President's house, St. Johns. It's painted bright yellow and has a dome.

Would R. take me, could we go, to the White House? He never tells me the rules, and I don't ask. I just see. Do they let Negroes in the front door? I wonder about the servants in the house. I hope they colored. The worst white folks in the world are the ones don't know any black folks at all—those up North with Irish maids.

Sweet day. R. had a touch of a cold, no fever, just a cough, but he didn't think it would be dignified to walk the halls of Congress hacking and spitting, so he canceled all his appointments and declared the day a Sabbath. Then he bathed, brushed, robed himself in striped silk, and spent it with me.

We played cards, whist, all afternoon, and all the cards seemed to fall my way. I feel lucky. Living in a hotel is like living in a tree, you are so far off the ground. I wonder how high up you have to be to get close to God. I wonder if anyone will ever design a place you can live as tall as the Washington Monument or, better still, as tall as the Washington Monument is going to be. If we are not living in the vicinity of God, I'm starting to think we are in the vicinity of low-flying angels.

There is a man staying in the hotel who is part of a delegation from Japan. He wants to know all about our home, the place where R. and I come from. In his lovely unlidded eyes, we are from the same place: "a plantation" in "the South." We are more alike each other than either of us is like him, more alike each other than either of us is like the people he knows from Boston. At least that's how it looks to him.

And this afternoon, with the cards falling my way,

holding all four queens: the diamond, the heart, the spade, and the club; hearing R. laugh with pleasure at my triumph as I placed my cards so they made a loud little sound smacking the table; as he laughed and announced, "And possessing a king too, you need no aces"; as we ate lunch sent up from the hotel restaurant, and I tasted just how different the world was than I thought it would be, how much larger it is than I thought it was—everything, everyone, and every place that wasn't in our suite seemed unreal. We played another hand of cards, and I let R. win.

47

*H*ard news from home—Other's gone. Other's gone. And now R.'s gone too, gone to bury his wife. Bad things come in threes. First the baby, then Mammy, and now Other. I thought he'd cry, but he didn't.

Now we won't have to wait for a divorce. Or maybe not. He's leaving here, he's leaving me.

There's the funeral and her first two children, the boy and the girl. At the door when he left he said that the children were his by law and conscience. He told me the children would keep living in her house in Atlanta. He'd be moving an English nanny in with them. Later he would send them to boarding school.

Gone. Fell down the steps. First came smallpox. They say she looked in the mirror, then fell down the steps. They say she'd been drinking.

R. got a wire; that's how we knew.

48

I was invited to the home of Mr. Frederick Douglass today. I'm not sure if I should go. R.'s not back yet. It's been a while. I've heard almost nothing from him. Nothing literate—only what Beauty and some of the home-folk scribbled. It's like a code. A code I've got to break before I know anything. First deciphering the letters, then puzzling out how the words, contorted by spelling, read, then trying to decide what these words, put together as they are, mean. Letters from Cotton Farm, dashed across scraps of paper, make my eyes want to snap shut. Beauty's chicken scratches embalmed in stale clouds of her perfume ache my head, reminding me that she's with him and I ain't. Reminding me that she knew him before I did. Quiet as I might keep it, maybe I wouldn't care so much if she knows him after I know him—except that loving him is the only work I'm trained to do. I would cry if it wouldn't make my eyes red, if dabbing at them wouldn't etch little chicken scratch lines into my skin that say, "Death's coming and it's catching." That's what the lines on a lady's face spell, and every man can read it.

No chickens will walk across her face while she sleeps. She will remain in the garden of his mind, and in mine, an early summer rose, before a petal is dropped, almost sweet, light-scented. He will never see her grow old. Nothing more than that thickening of waist, a dropping and thinning of bosom that had already begun, and a slight thickening of her nose and reddening of her face. She will live forever, in some Charleston-in-late-summer-on-the-Battery garden of his mind, blooming forever, showered by sweet wine.

I don't drink. Not much. Lady slapped the first glass of wine right out of my hand. I was thirteen. She was fierce. "Do you *want* to look like Planter?" I had no idea in this world what she was talking about, but I was so tickled I almost wet myself. "His face gets redder and his nose gets thicker every drink he takes. It happens to the Irish, and it'll happen to you." Just like that she said it, then ran her fingers through my hair. It was the first time I had heard her speak aloud that I was Irish, that I was his. Always before it had been a known, unspoken thing. And the moment Lady spoke it, the truth seemed less true. I don't know why, and I wished it wasn't. But the moment she spoke it, my truth became less mine. As she ran her fingers through my hair, I could feel her pulling away from my body; I heard and felt the truth being snatched away from me. I didn't see anything, but she could see Planter in me. And every day it was easier to see more of him in me, because every day she was coming to see other things in me she didn't like. And the more she saw what she didn't like, the more she could see Planter in me.

She was deserting me in little minutes, with small gestures, a half-combed curl, an unproffered glass of milk, a cast-aside field flower. That was it. I felt like a favored doll that had been sat back on the shelf after years between the pillows and the covers, just because a big blue box with white satin ribbon had arrived one cake-day and a prettier doll with raven curls had been pulled from the tissue paper. What I really felt like was the weed I had lovingly pulled from the yard and presented to her, only to find it later cast aside, untreasured, desiccated. It's a thirst-provoking recognition, the sight of yourself abandoned. It's how I got the wine glass in my hand, and Lady slapped it out. And it wasn't the wine glass that got slapped out of my hand; it was her love for me.

49

I had forgotten all this, how much things were changing at home then. Folks around here always talk about before the war and after the war. But for me, looking back, I divide it between when Other still lived under my mother's skirts and when she didn't. There came a time when Other was moving beyond Mammy, and that time cleaved our world.

Mammy still hacked a green apple clean in two with a wave of her kitchen knife, but when Other's little friends would come for a birthday, barbecue, or Christmas visit, she no longer cheerfully took them to Mammy's kitchen for play or for slices of apple dusted with cinnamon. No more did Mammy sit up and rock and scold in the room while the golden girls gossiped. Other's friends grew too old for Mammy to slap on the bottom and push into a room. They wanted baths drawn, darker hair combed, and dresses pressed. Without thought or malice, they ordered Mammy to perform these services. Other and I both watched this. We both heard the high-pitched, singsong, acid-sweet demands. It wounded us both, but it hurt her more.

Me, who had watched Other order Mama around all my life, was used to it. A beating you get regularly just don't hurt as much. Other was shamed for Mammy and she was scared for herself. All children live in a world of terrors. Cotton farms are scarier places than most. Smelling where the power lay, Other drew near the two muskiest people on the place—my mother and her father. Every single discovery of a weakness in my mother was another termite gnawing on the seasoned wood of her soul's foundation. And one day she kinda caved in. The day after that, she started building again.

If it was mine to speak over my sister's grave, I would remember this. First, she was afraid for Mammy—she hated the big blue life bruises Mammy suffered at the tiny hands of pale tyrants. She felt puny herself every time she was unable to protect Mammy. Then she hated Mammy for being hurt. When you can't protect a thing you love, it's natural to come to hate that thing a little bit more each and every time it's injured. Even if that thing is your Mammy's heart. Even if that thing is your daughter's body.

When Other got sick to death of all that hating, she decided the indignities were not so very awful. The lie worked. She forgave herself, she forgave the other little white girls who formed her circle of visitors, and she forgave Mammy.

Against her sisters and her closest friends, she claimed and held a grudge. Folk always found fault with Other for having precious few female friends. Mealy Mouth had aplenty; Other had few. Certainly it was true that most of Other's many enemies were female. But Other liked girls real good. I almost think the reason she loved Dreamy Gentleman so, was that there was so much boy in his man and so much girl in his boy. No, it would have been nearer to the truth to say Other didn't like to have anyone around who made Mammy's life a misery, and it was the girls close enough to demand intimate services that did the best job of that. Particularly her sisters. Particularly that bright beauty, China, whose beau she stole when she married Mealy Mouth's youngest brother. So she treated those girls, the ones who might have been her intimates, bad enough for them to stay away, stay clear, stay distant—from her, and stay distant from Mammy, stay distant from her and Mammy. The possibility of life without Mammy she did not consider.

If Other bore her discomfort with little grace, Mammy bore it with less. Mammy gained fifty pounds one year, forty the next, twenty the year after that, and the slight, barely hundred-pound body in which she had walked into the house and slipped into Planter's bed vanished beneath another hundred pounds of protective flesh. I believe Mammy felt Other pulling away from her, and she determined to pull away from Planter before he could pull away. Overnight, Mammy became a stout old woman of fifty.

Lady was ripe then, thirty, and maybe she was just a little hungry for what she hadn't known when Planter, stone drunk, ploughed into her stone-dry and laudanum-drugged body. She had felt no pleasure, had given no pleasure, felt no pain, gave no pain, as he flopped about, planting his seed in her soil. These were the days when she began to wonder if there might could be something more to these engagements. She was beginning to forget her girlhood.

At the same time Other was becoming uncomfortable with Mammy, she began to fall deeply in love with her mother, my Lady. I wanted to dash her brains out with a big rock. Other and Lady and Me. As they discovered each other, I discovered the higher temperatures of jealousy. The fever comes in different degrees. Other's love for Lady's tidy, tiny, sweet-smelling self, her slight but supple arms, the white, heaven–pillow bosom that lay corseted beneath Lady's modest gowns, brought sweat to my brow. It was a comfort to know, it remains a comfort to know, that Other died without ever once seeing her mother's breasts, breasts on which I sucked.

And Planter was beginning to see me anew. There was nothing strange between him and me. I was his daughter, and that meant more to him than it did to most men of his time and station when the daughter was brown. But the way he looked at me, Mammy didn't know if she was nervous or jealous. And not for the first time Lady felt the exact same thing.

Back then, I was hating Other so hard for breaking the

ribbons binding Lady to me that I noticed all of this, but I didn't weave it into the fabric of my understanding of my life. Yet circumstance has left me rich in time to think about those days. Not working is a severe affliction. If I had been turned out to field work, perhaps I would never have whipped up so hard on my own mind. But everything changed when Other fell out of love with Mammy and in love with Lady. Everything changed when Lady fell out of love with me. Everything changed when Planter noticed that I was some kind of cross between his wife and his woman. Everything changed, and they sent me away.

I could see in Other's face the first moment it came to her the possibility that Mammy did for her not because she wanted to, but because she had to. Maybe Mammy loved her and maybe Mammy didn't. Slavery made it impossible for Other to know. "She who ain't free not to love, ain't free to love." Some folks are easy with that and some folks are not. Mainly the folks who think they wouldn't be loved are easy with it.

What Lady did for me, she did freely. And what she did for Other was done that way too. So I for sure got something. I can't decide if I'm grateful that R. will finally never have to choose between us, between me and Other. Sometimes when I feel neither lucky nor worthy, I'm grateful to get the win any way I get it. Sometimes I can taste beating her out and I am sad to be starved of it.

Sometimes it feels like the game is over and I'm putting up the checkers, and instead of me winning, she just lost, or more like she never showed up. And that's something else altogether from the way I want to feel, triumphant! Winner-ly. However it happened, I'm just glad not to lose.

Other is dead, and I'm sorry for it.

50

I want to go to Mr. Frederick Douglass's house and I wouldn't be sorry to go without R. if I could go in propriety. I like moving among these Capital City Negroes. I met a young seamstress who mainly sews for white families, but she's going to do a bit of work for me. Rosie Woodruff is her name. There is something in this quick, trim African lady, something so city-like but clean that I had to drop my eyes to keep her from seeing that it was me who is admiring her. She wore a pitifully slim gold ring on her finger, and a skinnier brown-skin man was waiting for her at home, a plumber who came very lately from someplace deep South and had quick picked up a trade. Compared to this seamstress I have so much—or is it so little? Home feels far away. Every mile of the distance feels safe and getting safer. And every mile and hour it feels like something more of me is missing.

51

*T*oday I walked around the monument to President Washington. It's a half-finished thing, an odd white thumb coming up out of dirt and a few blades of grass, a stump of a thing, blasting through the dome of a cracked-in-two shell of sky.

The light in this city is so different from the light at the farm in Georgia, from the light in Charleston. The sky here is colored the blue of a robin's egg if the shell had been heated up with yolk-colored, straight-from-heaven sunrays. Always about me now is the sense of having died and gone to heaven.

Or died and gone to hell. Died for sure. There is a thickness to the Washington air. It's heavy with water and mosquitoes. I wear this air like a coat that keeps me from the cold I know is coming. And there's a thickness to the river. You can't see very deep into it for all that it carries, and it's wide. The Potomac seems to roll in here from someplace and curve slowly through the city like it's a good place to stay.

When I sailed to Europe I did not remember my fear of water until I was upon it for some days. Or was it Mammy's fear I remembered? Or Mammy's Mammy's fear? Where does fear go to become fascination? Is it where rivers go to become sea? More than anything I saw of Venice (gondolas, masks), of London (pints, a palace), of Paris (sewer rats, stained glass) after so much land, I saw all the rivers. The Potomac brings back to me a remembrance of rivers. A remembrance of rivers and river cities.

Walking along the streets I hear different languages. And the people dress differently not just because they are rich or poor but because the people of Atlanta dress differently from the people of Boston, who dress differently from the Philadelphians and there is a good bit of everybody roving 'round here.

In a way Washington, the Capital City, feels like an island. It belongs to nothing. I wonder what will be here in a hundred years? I wonder if anything will be here at all. The city is like a big pregnant woman lying on her side while everybody fans her and wonders when she's going to give birth. Or will the baby blast the life out of her, trying to press its way into life? We hear stories about the French L'Enfant and the black man, Banneker, who was his assistant, and how they were tossed out of their own vision, out of this town of their creation, for dreaming too wildly. Are there tame dreams? I wonder if this city with

its strange circles, somehow designed to make one can-
non do the work of six, but not generally sensible, I wonder if this city won't always be a kind of haint, struggling
to wake to the everyday needs of a struggling rural people, struggling to fall back into L'Enfant's grand dream
of a city of Senators and Ambassadors? Did he not understand our Congressmen were not so long ago farmers
and slaves? He didn't know that. I don't believe the Eu-
ropean ever fully understands the American. But this city
is built for tomorrow, and tomorrow I go the Douglasses'
for tea.

52

I went to the Douglasses' for tea. Their home is more
than a bit out of the way. Perched in the southeast quadrant of the city, high above a riverbank, Cedar Hill re-
wards the adventurous sojourner with a superb view
across the Anacostia to the Federal city.

It's a new kind of home for me. There was a comfortable expanse but no formality—in the architecture. The
formality was in the language, and now I borrow it for
mine.

Was this the first party in my life I had attended alone,
unescorted? Has any other woman in the world arrived

at a formal party on her own? I surprised myself by going; I surprised a few of the other guests, I expect. And I was glad I did, from the moment a gap-toothed girl with an intelligent smile, gold-rimmed glasses, and long puffy-kinky hair opened the door and waved me in to join the crowd.

The party revolved around an immense cut-glass punch bowl filled to the brim with what tasted to be a mixture of fruit juice and tea. This bowl sat in the middle of a draped round table in a square entry hall. There were no big crystal bowls of flowers and no waiters, just shining faces and everyone helping themselves.

In the corner of the drawing room three young women from Fisk University in Nashville gave an impromptu rendition of "Soon I Will Be Done with the Troubles of the World," and this afternoon I felt I wouldn't have to leave this earth for it to be true.

We, Frederick Douglass and I, barely exchanged three sentences, but he looked at me as they sang, and I could see that he liked what he saw. As I was making my way through the crowd (so many sky-blue, so many cardinal-colored gowns—the effect—due to the new dyes—was quite unintentionally patriotic) after the song, twice the great man nodded as he smiled in my direction.

I never got too close to Douglass again, but I enjoyed a lively conversation with his son. I enjoyed this party. It was a kind of Negro open house, the kind of event to which I am not frequently invited. Mulatto mistresses of Confederate aristocrats have little standing in Negro society. And the Congressman was there.

God was showing off the day He created the Congressman. He is that good-looking. Or maybe God was just taking a stand. Who will deny the humanity of such a body, such a mind?

When the Congressman raised my hand to his lips, to kiss in greeting, I shook so hard, I was embarrassed. I flushed. I don't remember what words he said. But he offered me his arm, and we walked together into the Douglasses' garden. As we walked, he talked. He said some surprising things.

The girls from Fisk, teased again into song, had launched into "Go Down, Moses." I was amazed by their performance — the haunting combination of the raw and the refined. I told him so.

"Be not amazed," chastised the Congressman. "Be not amazed."

"They will amaze the Queen. Why not me?"

"Who is Victoria compared to you? You've seen more than she. We see it daily. We are the chosen ones, the ones who sometimes snatch victory from the jaws of tragedy."

"To what tragedy do you refer?"

"Do you require a particular tragedy?" For a moment he allowed himself the pleasure of being amused by the rhetorical question; then he waxed earnest. "Until it is transformed by our own energy, our own muscle, our own brain, every second of our very existence on these shores is tragic."

I hated hearing those words. I wanted to put my hand on his mouth and whisper, *"Hush."* Like I was Mama and he was Baby. But he's a man and I'm no mother, and he just kept talking. "And once transformed, *even the least little bit,* one drop of transformation, in the entire body of a life, makes the life victorious."

He touched the hard round muscle in the top of my arm, that golden hill of my inheritance, legacy of my childhood labor. Then he kissed his fingertips and pressed the kiss to my arm.

The release was as powerful as a little death on the green velvet couch. I was tired and wanting to hear more. He told more: "Just like one drop of blackness in the entire body of a man make him black."

What would it be like to have a drop of him in me? To keep from fainting, I changed the subject and gave him my most frozen smile.

Now he talked to me of the events of the day, expecting me to be proud of his accomplishments. I didn't know enough of the events of the day to truly value his part, but I knew enough of men to value the way he held hisself—the way even Douglass deferred to him and leaned closer to hear what the Congressman had to say when he allowed his voice to drop down low.

In that moment, the very moment Douglass leaned toward him to claim some word of his as their secret, I wondered if the Congressman could be mine. And I laugh at myself for wondering. I have been R.'s, but no one had ever been mine. I have never possessed a man. I had never hoped to possess a man. Never even wished to possess a man's soul, for it seemed too close to slaving. But now I am wondering if he could be mine, and if I knew if he could be mine, I might attempt possession. And wondering if I could possess the Congressman (as I turned away from him, all the time stealing sideways glances back at him, while moving back toward Douglass's son) raises the possibility of me possessing R.

Everything about ownership is changing: land, people, money, gold into foreign currency, foreign currency back into foreign gold, and gold back into money in our banks. It doesn't seem in this time of hurricanes and storms and other acts of God, with winds of every sort of change in the air, that hearts would be any different. Why couldn't she who couldn't own, who now owned forty acres and a mule—if I could own a former plantation—could I not own a planter's heart?

R. needs to get home soon. I've sent him a note. "I need what a man who's gone can't do. I love you. Speed your return." I wrote those words in my head while I was looking at Douglass, looking at the Congressman, and some young fool was mumbling to me. Could he, either he, which he, if both could be mine, who would I have? Could I have either?

But the gap-toothed girl, now in a cloak, caught the Congressman's eye, and he moved away, leaving the party with only a distant bow in my direction. And I was left to lesser pleasures of observation.

The dresses were modest and trim; there was an abundance of simple good food. Plates were eaten off laps on stairs after folk were seated on every available chair. Many of the young gentlemen stood.

Douglass has traveled to England and has many English friends. One English gentleman referred to the streamers down the back of a rather saucy bonnet as "follow-me-my-lads," and the back porch burst into laughter as the brown girl in question gaily skipped across the lawn. These are new and lighter days.

Several of the visitors were students at Howard University. Some, as I have already written, were visiting from down South.

I am trying to suck it all in deeply. Trying to feel how this place feels different from the farm when all the white folks were away. That's when we had our holiday, not Christmas. There were times when all of them went to Atlanta or Savannah or Charleston, when the overseer was suddenly taken sick up in bed. Strange how overseers so often took sick when the family was away during the holidays. That is when we had our Christmas.

And now it should be Christmas every day, but it is not. What it is, is the days before. Working, getting ready. Everything now is expectation, hope, waiting for Christmas to come but we don't know when.

53

*T*his morning I went out walking in my new neighborhood, Georgetown, and I came upon Tudor Place. It's just a house. Just another rich man's house, but I wanted to weep. Weep for beauty, weep for home, weep for not believing Garlic when he told about all the places he had been and what he had seen. Here was the model for our round porch with columns. Here a different variation of the theme of five portions. Garlic's building, Tata, is much more beautiful. It's not just what will they let us be; it's what will we let ourselves be.

I wish I was a man and I could vote. I'd be a man if I could vote now. So much of who we will let ourselves be will be decided by who we will vote for and will we vote and how long will they let us vote.

There's a cartoon I cut out of *Harper's Weekly*. I'm looking at it now. It's a drawing of Jefferson Davis, him that was the President of the Confederacy, Davis, with a big cloak wrapped all around him. His face is long and thin, his eyes so dark, when you glance at the drawing it looks like a skull with a hat and hair, like a skeleton wearing a cloak. And this Jefferson—I like to call him by his first name—he looks like a figure on stage, like a demon sneaking off to do wrong, except he's in the center of the picture, but off to the side *is* the center of *this* picture, and Jeff, he was standing there, looking back into the Senate chamber at a Negro man taking his seat, his Senate seat. A deep dark Negro man surrounded by compatriots is what it looked like. And the Negro man is reading. His hands are on one book, and another book has slid off his table to the floor at his feet. He's propped up and on books. His colleagues are turned to question him, and he's ready.

That's what it looked like to me. There's a caption: TIME WORKS WONDERS. I do not know if it was meant to be for or against this dark legislator. Certainly it was the truth. Under that title was written the words of Iago, and between Iago's name and his speech was inserted, in parentheses, the name "Jeff Davis." I read *Othello* again after I saw this cartoon. The speech says, "For that I do suspect the lusty Moor hath leapt into my seat: the thought whereof both like a poisonous mineral gnaw my inwards." If I had been Othello's friend, Desdemona would still be alive, and they'd have plenty of pretty babies.

Othello's just a creation. Maybe just like me. But

Robert B. Elliott be real. He be born in Massachusetts. He studied at Eton College in England and now he's in the Congress. Robert B. Elliot be real and my Congressman knows him. James Rapier studied in Canada and now he's in Congress. He's another "historical figure." And my Jeems, his beloved Smalls, I've found all about him now, for Jeems's sweet sake. Smalls was wholly self-educated and wholly factual. He taught himself to read and write. How you do that? John Roy Lynch, he worked in a photographer's studio and he looked across an alley into a white schoolroom and followed his lessons from a distance right into the Mississippi house and on into the Congress of these United States. He merits a line in anybody's history of these United States. But it's one thing to read about them and quite another to smell a man's scent, hear his quicker mind responding to your own quick thought. Tick-tock. It's an altogether different thing.

There are facts can poison you dead as arsenic. I have long known this to be true. There are facts can get you drunker than sipping whiskey straight. This is a sweet and new discovery. *O brave new world!* Sweet Jesus! Let me know some more about it! Please God!

54

R.'s returned. He looks a thousand years old. His hair is turning white, and he has let it grow long. This is a Southern city, but he doesn't fit in here. He strides about in black silk and velvet and looks like the ghost of the Confederacy, a sauntering relic haunting the place. Like the evil Godmother at the baby's christening. Why do I write that? I feel like the princess who is cursed at birth. And they try to change the curse, try to move her to safety. Why does R. look like the evil Godmother? Who looks like the prince? Who does R. look like?

His face looks so different in this light. I call out to myself, "Who is this man I lay with?" and I have no response. This man is unknown to me. Perhaps even unknowable by me. And maybe that is exactly what I love about my man. Not knowing him feels so familiar, as familiar as the smell of whiskey, and leather, and horses, and a certain cologne, yes. He is the stuff of Lady's dreams, my dark-eyed gambler and arrogant risk-taker. The arrogance was essential ...

If he has anything to say to me, he should just say it.

55

*O*ne of our Senators, a gentleman from the Eastern Shore of Maryland, sent a bushel basket of Chesapeake Bay oysters 'round to the townhouse in honor of R.'s return last evening. People heard that he had a wife and that she died. Neither of us was hungry for supper, so we ate the oysters for breakfast.

He said I looked like a mermaid. I said he looked like King Neptune. He did look just like some briny sea god, with a mud-caked shell in his fingers, sucking down the juice after the plump-jiggle slid down his throat. I had to smile at him, and smile at the memory of wanting him to slide down my throat. My desire for him had been so much more than distraction or work. Once upon a time I was as hungry for him as today we are hungry for breakfast.

Love and desire are not the same thing. Most often they don't even live in the same house. They should but they don't. He promised me a trip back across the water, to Europe, a grander tour, ensemble, together. He didn't see me shudder.

For his teeth were finding a pearl just at that moment. He plucked it from his mouth with his fingers. The pearl was blue when you looked at it one way and gray when you looked at it in another. It was very small and not so

exactly round. He balanced it on the tip of his pointer finger, and I snatched it with my tongue and swallowed.

I want to surprise him. At least once again. I want to
insist without words that we will not just be restless, and
prosperous, and contained. I want to have more than a
liquor bottle to keep me in my skin, to keep me in my
house. Once he could rock me into my skin, rock me out
of my imagination into the marrow of my bones. He did
that for me and I remember it. Will every kiss I kiss be in
remembrance of him, who he used to be?

I swallowed the pearl, and tears appeared in his eyes,
tears I had never seen before. He knows our passion plays
hide-and-seek with us now. Rain falls in our hearts. Rain,
rain, go away! Cindy and R.B. want to play! Oysters are
no breakfast food.

As if in sympathy, it began to rain outside. After
breakfast I went to my room to write a letter to Beauty, a
letter full of gloom. "It's raining now. Heaven's tears are
washing over us. In the Capital City this is the sacrament
that substitutes for breakfast with Beauty..." I had just
written those words when R. walked into my room without knocking.

He kissed me on the back of the neck and dropped a
pack of letters onto my little desk. I asked him what it
was. A smile curled onto his lips, sharp and tight, as dangerous a curve as the curve of my breasts. Sneering, he
was an especially good-looking man; nastiness brought a

flash of "earlier days" across his face. I had to tell myself to breathe, because he took my breath away. He flicked that packet onto my desk in a manner these city Negroes might call "hincty," something akin to but different from "uppity," with a studied nonchalance that barely covers insolence and smells of fear.

For the first time, in all the time I had known him, he was trying too hard. The gesture was, as the Creoles (who, though few and far between in number, lend their great charm to this city, when they can be found) say, *"un peu trop,"* just a little too much. Or were all his gestures that way and I just was seeing it for the first time? Certainly this gesture was *de trop* and his words were the cherries on the cake. "Your manumission papers," he said, without hurting me at all.

He walked out of the room without saying another word.

They were love letters. The letters Lady had written to Cousin and the letters he had written to her. I had heard from Miss Priss that Lady, in her delirium on her deathbed, had called out someone's name. It was hard to hear what she was saying, but Miss Priss thought she was calling Feleepe, the name of her cousin who had been killed in the duel. The cousin who died in New Orleans just before Lady married. Lady herself had told me some little about him. Once, even, holding me in her arms, she had laughed and cried, laughed and cried, rocking me back and forth, kissing my head, whispering, "I wish you were my child, I wish you were my child." I thought very little about it. I had so long and feverently wished for Lady to be my mother, her wish sounded to my ear only natural and true. It's hard, having natural wishes in an unnatural time.

There is no difficulty in deciphering these letters. Each of them wrote a beautiful hand. Each was urgently trying to convey information of supreme importance, and they felt safe, so their sentences ran frankly naked. Lady and Cousin were beautiful children, bold and unhurt. For a time, in the early pages, that untested boldness served them as bravery and lent clarity to every utterance. Later, when I knew her, Lady's every utterance was dressed, and all meaning obscured and distorted, the way her body was obscured and distorted by whalebones and hoops and cinches and pantalets and all manner of torturous frippery. But at the first all was plain and simple.

56

P——,

I add no dear or darling, your name alone is prayer! I tremble in fear of God's judgment, for I know I am guilty

of idolatrous worship—of you. How can I love God with all my heart when I have no heart? You have my heart. I beg you to go to church on Sunday, for it is the only way my heart can go and I may see you there. Ask Daddy soon. I am not too young. And Mother loves you so. I hear her call, her greeting, "Sweet son of own departed sister." How she does go on, Mamma. This house is neither cool enough nor hot enough. Take me away from it to some place where the air is not the temperature of my skin—where mosquito bites are not the only thing I feel.
E

———

Dearest Girl, Darling E———,
Dearest and darling are your name. Belonging to you alone. There are other Elizabeths, other Emilys, other E———s, but there is only one dearest girl, you. I shall give you fire and ice when we are married. I'll rub ice on your wrists in July and build great big fires in December. Don't you swoon. P.

P.
Mother found your last letter and took to weeping. "What does he mean, what does he mean?" When I tried to explain, she interrupted me, saying, "Oh, it's all too clear, all too clear." I have no idea what she's so upset

about. You should ask Daddy at once. I think they don't believe you really want to marry me.
Your E.

———

My dear E———,
Your father refuses to let me marry you. I asked him to state his reservation, and he could say only that your mother disapproves of the match. I must talk to my Aunt. P.

———

P.
Mother does nothing but cry. She took me on her lap and whispered, between sobs, "If it was possible, I would allow it." If I do more than bow in your direction at church, she will remove me from the city. She says the curse of Haiti is upon us.

P., what does Haiti have to do with this? I have my little income from there and you have yours. It should buy us a little freedom. This all sounds like a nightmare my old Mammy used to tell me about ill-used slaves coming to haunt families that were cruel to them. Sometimes they scared the people so bad, their hearts beat right out of their chests, then stopped beating at all. E.

Darling,
Your mother, my aunt, refuses to see me at all. I'm just about to go to the graveyard to talk with my mother. P.

E.
You must write. It's been days since I spoke with you. I come to your house and am refused entrance. Have the gates of hell opened and swallowed you whole? P.

P.
What do you know of Haiti? I don't believe I've ever seen it on a map. I don't believe I'll ever take another tea-spoon of sugar in my life. Mother doesn't know that I know why she believes we can't marry. The reason doesn't constrain me. Doesn't shackle my heart from yours. But my tongue is locked in the prison of my mouth. You would have to make your own decision, and I do not know what you would decide, and if I tell you what I know, you will never be yourself again, and if I do not tell you, we will never be what we might be. If you wish to know, send word and I will tell you. Your cousin E.

Darling E.

Was our great-grandmother a murderess? Did she kill a hundred slaves because one displeased her? I refuse to be afraid or ashamed of decades-old indiscretions of my progenitors. Tell me at once, and I will be as I remain, who I am, the man who wants to marry you. P.

———

P.

Our great-grandmother was not a murderess. She was a Negresse. E.

———

Dear E.———,

I am surprised you put those words to paper. I am proud of you, very proud, and I should still like to marry you. I spoke with Aunt. Your mother sees no life for us that will not destroy the rest of the family. She says her confinement and the confinement of her sister, my mother, were agony, greatly lessened but not ended by the arrival of perfect pink infants. She says they watched the tips of our ears and ridge of skin around our fingers every night for signs of darkening. I asked her what she would have done if she had seen the tip of your ear turn the color of one of the walnuts just falling. Even if you had turned the color of butter, if she had turned the color of butter, I would have put the pillow on her face and I would have cried. Color comes in so slow over a period of ten days, if you do it quick even the Daddy don't see the dark in the baby. Of course the Mammy knows. They've seen all manner of white-looking nigger children. What farce this is. It's a pity Molière didn't live in this city and this part of the country. Instead of writing the Imaginary Invalid, he could have written the...what would we call ourselves? Niggers Who Knew Not? Can you be a Negro if you don't know you're a Negro? I would have said a nigger knows he's a nigger. Always. Absolutely. But what if he doesn't? So...we are each to pour a little more milk in the coffee and not tell. We were the ones who were not supposed ever to know—the first to be white not black with a secret. See how well our love serves us. If we had not fallen in love, we might never have discovered our darkness. P.

———

P.——— Write to me. I know you're in New Orleans. Everyone says you're drinking too much, fighting, dueling with anyone willing to walk across your shadow. You said you would never marry anyone but me—but you did not say you would marry me. Of course I wish I did not know what I know now. I wish I was not what I am now, but if I had to do it over again and I could either stay innocent or love you and hold for a minute the possibility of being your bride, I would choose knowledge and agony over innocence and no hope of marrying you. Could we not go someplace where no one knows us and be who we are? E.

———

Dear E.

Strange as it may seem, it is not as hard for me to imagine having a Negresse for my bride as it is for me to imagine you having a Negro for your husband and in your bed. It feels blasphemous. Even when I know the Negro so well and know his desire for you to be as hot and pure as fire. If you will marry me, I will marry you when I return. Perhaps we will move to a plantation down in the Indies. I have been sniffing around for possibilities down here. Port cities are good for possibilities. P.

———

Inside the last of the envelopes were two folded yellowing newspaper articles. One told the story of a deadly duel between hotheaded dandies down in the Quarter. The other the story of the premature death of a well-loved son of Savannah under mysterious circumstances. Same story, different tellers; only the fact of death remained.

57

*O*ther never knew. R. received the letters from Garlic; he got the letters from Mammy. She got the letters from Lady. How Lady came to possess both sides of the most important correspondence of her life is not hard to imagine—she kept those he sent her and, rather than destroy anything her hand had touched or risk disclosure, he had returned hers to her. I could only imagine how many times Lady had read and re-read the words that did and didn't change her life. The pleasure must have been exquisite for her, to take so much risk with her daughters' lives, to risk the damage "an unveiling" would have done to her life. I can only imagine that when she handed the letters to Mammy, she expected Mammy to burn them. She expected the secret her mother never wished to tell her to die with her. She left her daughters to carry their babies without fear of their own children darkening up.

They're walking over my grave again. I know why Precious cried in the night. I remember finding the clothespin in her bed, the lemon oil on her elbows. I know all about whitening up; they did what they could for me.

I wonder why Garlic gave R. the letters. I wonder if he knew what they contained. He didn't read or write, and he wasn't a man to think words were important. I'll have to ask him, but I'm guessing that he left the letters for R. out of simple honesty, out of a desire to give him a gift. What a strange moon we are under. With this gift what has he robbed R. of? Or perhaps it was simple spitefulness.

Mammy might have told Garlic what the letters contained. He was too careful a man to let them be read by just anybody. If he had been curious, he would have asked me to read the letters to him. I don't believe he paid any attention to them at all. The letters were not the only things R. brought back with him from Cotton Farm. He also brought me a ring.

It was stone-less gold band without ornamentation. Inscribed on the underside were Lady and Feleepe's initials. R. raised my hand to his lips; I thought he was going to kiss it. Instead, he slipped the Charleston ring from my finger and dropped it into his watch pocket.

Old light, some yellow light, almost an ancestral light, flickered in R.'s eyes, now framed by creases, a hundred crinkling curved lines that changed, creating a sparkling effect as he dropped to his knee. He was slow and unsteady as he lowered himself, but he was certain of his destination. He looked like what he was—a courtier from an age gone by. I found the effect of effort wed to a feebleness endearing. Gallantry is never so visible as when it is doomed. I had a portrait in my mind of R.—a portrait of prosperity and beneficence—but a new portrait was forming in my mind—the portrait of a lonely man. The more he resembled this new portrait, the closer I came to falling in love with him.

58

The Congressman sent me flowers and a note that R. found charming. R. thanked me for helping him "cultivate" his "new friend." I let him think I was doing him a favor. The flowers were yellow roses and they reminded me of home. As I re-read these pages—and I do that more often than I write new ones these days—I find myself looking backward. I spent most of my life looking toward the front room of my life, toward escape or change, toward some new way to be, some new place to stand, some new person to stand with. And now, thirty years into my life, my life half over, I am always looking backward, trying to rearrange my memories, rearrange and dust, celebrate and protect, all those antique memories, sticks that came into the house of my mind without me paying them no mind at all, sticks that have become my treasure.

How is that? Once when I lived looking forward, I never thought about me or allowed myself to feel anything but pleasure or joy. It was a kind of trick. My special trick; all other feelings provoked an immediate invisible sleep. I appeared to be awake but I was gone and dreaming. It was a satisfying trick, and I performed it like a circus dog. I never remembered anything unkind, never remembered or indulged my jealousy. Living in my own little house which R. visited in Atlanta, I swept all darkness away immediately under the rug of my springy bangs. And now someone's pulled the rug away. In fact, I find more hair in my brush every day than I wish, and all those things I swept away have shown themselves to still be there. And I have no idea in the world what to do with those unpleasant memories.

How is it that the South, the world of chivalry and slavery and great white houses and red land and white cotton, is gone, forever gone, in the dust, blown off and away, and it is only in me and my memories and in my soul-carving fear that the Southland lives on? Carved or seared on my heart, why does it seem so completely unobscurable? Why do I remember what can never help me? Why do I remember my world better than I remember myself? So much I know about what I saw; so little I know about my own eyes. I'm tired. My bones are starting to ache. The butterfly sleeps softly crimson on my brown face, and I will sleep well tonight.

59

*W*as it just this morning we ate oysters for breakfast? I don't feel very well. I wonder if swallowing the pearl will kill me. It can't be the oysters. R. ate them too, and he feels fine. An old melody I made up in Cotton Farm days floats on the waves of nausea to the front of my brain. "The moon's all worn out and silver, trying to climb up the hill. The moon is just a sliver, I believe it never will. The moon I want to wish on, I'm waiting for it still." The moon that hangs outside the brick-faced window of our Georgetown townhouse is a worn-out sliver. I feel as exhausted as it looks. I hum the old melody and realize that I have hummed it before, because he, padding toward me in his silk dressing gown, is humming it too.

He came to me in the bed and we comforted each other. His white hair falling on my shoulder. I kissed his hairy ears and his crepe-y neck, I stroked his prosperity-swollen belly. He strokes the almost flat, still firm flesh of my stomach, and I wonder if I am going to have a baby. Sometimes morning sickness doesn't just come in the morning.

I never had any idea why no baby had come. It was just an unasked-for unthanked blessing. I have no hope. I hold no illusion that he would cradle my baby the way he cradled hers. I believe, I believed, I will continue to believe, that he loves me more than he loved her. That he loved me first and fiercer, that the very first time he saw her what drew him in was not her love for the fey one, the ephemeral boy-man, Dreamy Gentleman, but it was that she looked so much like me, looked like me but was a bright light-of-the day possibility. Dreamy Gentleman was the man his father and Charleston thought they wanted R. to be. Other was the prize to win that would prove He was more than He. But that is not why he wanted her; he wanted her as an echo of me. But I know this, this I remember, the men don't love the brown babies as they love the pale white ones.

60

*M*aybe some men do. I think of Garlic and how he never showed Other the fondness he showed me. I think of Mr. Frederick Douglass; he seemed proud indeed of his Ambassador son. I wonder about the Congressman. There's not much to wonder, is there? I blush to think of his happiness were he ever to discover his seed growing in my belly. I am not with child. I saw it this morning. I wonder if I can still make a baby. If I could ever make one. I never bled too much. We who clean the sheets and drawers know all about blood and talk about it too. You clean the sheets, you know a lot of things. It was never mine to wash the sheets at the plantation, but I washed my many at Beauty's; I am coming to feel I am a sheet-washing woman, a prelude to birth, a handmaid to birth, but not the creator herself.

I know he can have babies, because he gave Other one. I want a little loaf of my own rising in the oven. I cannot stay in this city here with him. It's too much. I have accepted the injustice of all of them loving her different because she was white. If she was just a nigger like me but got the chance to live white, it's too much to bear. But maybe that's just the way it is, so I'm broke. Right in half.

61

She was just a nigger. Their baby was just a high-yellow gal in a blue velvet riding habit. It's like she's died again. I ask him what it all means to him, and he makes a joke of it and says, "I guess they're right. Once you go black, you don't go back." He said that to me and I laughed, but he didn't think it was funny and I didn't either.

Lady. Lady love. Lady my love. Mamalady. What does it mean, river deep and summer green to me, that you are black and he was black, and you still wanted to marry him, and have his little may-be-brown babies? Could you have loved me just that much and I didn't know it? Was it always there for me to suck in on the tip of your pap and I didn't taste it, in your eye when you watched Other? In your eye when you watched Planter? The trick you played on him. And what about the trick you played on me? That I was one flavor and she was—other —and better than me? Other and better than my mother?

There was a day you almost told me. I must have been about six years old. Too old to be carried or lifted anymore. Old enough for more little jobs. You pronounced me "herb finder." When the overseer complained to Planter, "You wife is making a pet out of that pickaninny" and Planter tried to embarrass you by quoting the overseer's charges, you lied without hesitation, "Every fine family in Savannah has one, and what precisely does our overseer know about the care and feeding of a tribe of Southern aristocrats?" You held your chin up in the air when you said that; you let your voice shake with pride of birth. The husband could see for himself the blue blood pulsing in the vein of his wife's temple.

Planter was petrified and chastened. He didn't move a finger, blink an eye; it was as if he had turned to stone. The unspoken word "pineswamppeckawood" hung in the air, an invisible syllabic sword of Damocles, and he'd be damned if it fell on his head. He would not stand too close to the overseer. For all his Planter swagger, for all his luxurious clothes, for all his acres, his only genuine link to the aristocracy was his lady, whose lily-white "quality" hand seemed raised to draw a line that placed him on the trash side of the social divide.

All white skins are not created equal; he knew that; and I learned it as I watched them engage in the only argument of their marriage. That he had offended the dignity of magnolia maidenhood and made his lady fainting mad was obvious. He had sinned against the only creed he had sworn to, the credo of milady's fragility, the creed that balanced the vow to protect the particular delicate needs of particular delicate ladies against all the ugly peculiar Southland customs. He let her win—then resumed his place at the victor's side. When the word "peckawood" fell, it was on the overseer's head—right out of Planter's mouth.

After that I was the official herb finder. When guests came to call, I would busy myself with this occupation and thus be away from the house, away from prying eyes, insolent mouths. When the visitors were gone, Lady and I would have dignified reunions in which she would inspect my bounty. Lady would draw pictures of what she wanted me to find. Sometimes when guests would stay a length of days, she would send me out with a long list and I would make a kind of camp down near the cabins and stay away until I had assembled all the specimens.

With my bounty she would make little sachets and cures. There was a sachet she made for her own pillow that helped her fall asleep.

I seldom wore shoes and never on these rambles. I was proud of the calluses on my feet that allowed me to move nimbly and quickly over the farm; the calluses on my feet were the only part of my body I found superior to Other's. When my color deepened in the summer, I envied her more.

One day, at the end of an unusually long midsummer expedition, I was passing near the cabins when some of the "chil'rin" started teasing me, saying, "You done ripened right up," "'Bout time to pick her," "Think she'll fall from the tree herself," "Juicy—fruit, juicy-fruit." I ran back home, crying all the way.

But I didn't drop my herbs.

Later that night Lady took me down to where some poor white folks lived. A baby was due at their house and they had no money for a doctor, and even if they had, there weren't none about. She took me on the pretense of needing someone to tote her things into the house.

When we were alone I told her I wished I was white like her. I told her that I hated the color of my skin. She made a list of everything that was brown and beautiful in the world. She named walnut shells and fall leaves. She named tree bark and caramel. She named molasses, she named syrup, she named golden honey and sweet butter, the top of a cornbread, and finally she named the heel of a loaf of white bread. She was still naming and I was still crying, only harder. She opened her mouth to speak. She said, "I'm…I'm…I'm tired, and we need to go back home."

Then she took Feleepe's ring, the ring I wear as I write this, from the bodice of her dress, where it lay knotted into a handkerchief. I had seen it on her finger a time or two when we were alone. She took the ring and pressed it into the palm of my hand. The day I left Cotton Farm I pressed it back into her palm.

Garlic told R. that Mammy gave him the ring. She say Lady gave her the ring. Mammy say she want Garlic to give the ring to R. and she wanted R. to give the ring to me.

My mother, her Mammy. I never had a name to call her that I was fond of. Can you give somebody a name after she's in the ground? Can you hear me, Mama? Do you know which one of you I am calling? Black mama, white mama. Narrow mama, wide mama. None of that is anything. Mama I knew and Mama I didn't. I wonder if Mammy didn't see me as something like a Benedict Arnold, looking and telling all she see. Never learning the rule of silence. The rule of talk talk talk and don't tell nothing. Just the opposite of Lady, who spoke so little and said so much. Let me be greedy. I hope when I die I go to heaven. I know both my Mamas are praying for me.

I expect, if I get to heaven, the first sound I'll hear is the sound of Mammy's crimson petticoat, the rustle of her heavenly garment moving toward me. We're going to a ball tonight. I'm going to wear rustling taffeta of my own.

62

*T*hree days ago R. handed me an opened envelope addressed to him, along with unopened letters addressed to me. Inside his envelope was a stiff cream-colored card edged in gold, covered all over in flowing black writing. He was invited to attend a ball; he was invited to bring a guest. A ball on Massachusetts Avenue. He invited me to join him.

The host has a long unpronounceable name with many consonants, but I am practicing pronouncing it in preparation for my part in honoring the visiting dignitary from Russia. Rosie says she can finish the bronze taffeta just in time. R. says I must not look too pretty, or an impoverished Count will attempt to carry me back to his crumbling-down castle beneath the snows of Siberia.

We rode to the ball in R.'s new carriage. I wore the new gold velvet cape with which R. surprised me this morning. We are becoming Washingtonians.

Some visitors to the Capital City refer to Massachusetts Avenue as Embassy Row. Many of the streets
in Washington are named after states. The wide main
streets in the middle of the city are named after important states. The White House is located on Pennsylvania
Avenue. Virginia Avenue supports the banks of the Potomac. There's nothing of importance on Georgia Avenue, nothing at all.

I was not prepared for the Embassy. It's a citified building, ornate and fortress-like, gray and tall, with narrow
windows. Of course there is no porch, there is no drive.
There's a gate, a wall, and then the street. We are in a
world city, and world cities exclude before they separate.

Music and candlelight illuminate the general darkness
of the large and drafty room. White-skinned, white-
gloved servants pass trays of champagne and odd little
bits and pieces of smoked fish and boiled eggs decorated
with piped mayonnaise and bits of chopped vegetable. A
waiter who speaks no English offers me a serving of
caviar and I say, "I would love a silverspoon of inky, fishy,
gray-black grits." Champagne spurts from R.'s mouth.
We are laughing together between nibbles of caviar on
toast.

I tell him that Russian princesses live in crumbling-
down villas, not palaces. He is pleased with me.

R. talks at the gentlemen and I dance with them;
dance with the one he's not talking at.

I like the swirl. It's the swirl I like. The swinging round in circles, the bouncing back and forth, the swirl. The way the colors blend and streak, the way the music gets louder and softer as you swing closer to it and away. Though I wear a gown of bronze, it appears that lilac is the color of the season. It's here in every shade: shiny lilac and muted lilac, bluer lilac and grayer lilac, lilac almost silver and lilac turning into purple. Beaded lilac and lilac brocade. And here and there the new shade of blue and the new shade of red. The swirl. The way it's just like eyes-wide-open dreaming. I would dance with any feet in shoe leather.

The candles burn down. The band gets louder and lazier. I twirl with some gentleman from Boston, a former abolitionist, come to Washington to help create the new national university. I believe it's called, or to be called, the Smithsonian Institution. R. talks to someone from Treasury. "What can he be saying now?" my dance partner teases. I would blush, but the red's already on my face. The butterfly. What is he saying now?

Something he's said before and before. Something he's said before. That's what he says now. And he won't hear what's being said now. There's money to be made after the war. Each year it seems a little more. There's money to be made after the war, but R.'s not making very much of it. He doesn't feel the tides the way he did, or the wind. He doesn't listen the way he did. He's somewhere else all the time now, responding to new acts with old gestures fragilely bridging past to present, ending his span before the future is reached.

Of course, he made money during the war and before the war. Why is it called that way? Collected money, gathered money, from where it had been, resting or clinched, into a grand green pile somewhere behind the doors of his bank. All those words would be better than "made." Behind the door of his bank is a place R. has never taken me. It's the only remaining place I know of for sure.

This gentleman from the Smithsonian is asking me if I knew that James Smithson, the man whose will left the money to start the Smithsonian Institution, if I knew James was illegitimate. "He was born James Lewis Macie. He took his father's name only after his mother died." I smile and start listening a bit more attentively. I didn't know this and it does interest me. He says James's mother was an English lady. It's good to know the daughters of English gentility have illegitimate children too. "The times are changing. Barriers are falling," he says mid-spin. But I'm thinking: I know dimly of clubs and weddings, lines across which no colored can step. Not even me with he. He goes to places I cannot go.

And I'm still playing pronoun games. Who is object; who is subject; is it me, or am I it?

Someone has tapped on the shoulder of the Smithsonian fellow, and I never discover how Macie became Smithson; my waist is released from his vise. The music slows down. I'm in the arms of the dark prince, my Congressman. My new partner and I move in a glorious syncopation. I stop wondering about the places I cannot go and go. This is the first territory into which I have entered into which R. cannot follow.

Prancing across the floor with the Congressman, I hold in my breath, press the back of my tongue against the roof of my mouth to make my chin, my throat, look taut. I want him to see me like I used to be. I want him to confuse the past with the present. I want the past and the future to fuse. I want to scare my Congressman into believing the things I believe about the future. I want to possess him. What would it mean to make him mine? By what skill would I achieve the capture? Is it more than that? I want him to want me. And it's so hard to tell if he does.

He whispered strange stories into my ear. "My Daddy," says he, "had such a headache, my Mama hit him upside the head with a skillet, and I popped out, full dressed in overalls, ready to pick a day's cotton—just so Mama could take a day's rest."

"I don't believe you."

"Find a record that proves me wrong. A birth certificate. A baptism sheet. Anything."

"It's tragic those things don't exist."

"I've told you what I think of tragedy."

I wanted to hit him upside the head, but I didn't have a skillet.

When I was short and lived on the farm, I knew my way to a field of exotic wild verbena with orange-colored flowers and lemon scent. They were favorites of Lady's, but this verbena looked like another wild herb that was poisonous. You could tell the difference by looking at the petals—one had tapered petals and one had squat squared petals. I no longer remember which was which. Things I thought I would never forget I have forgotten. Things I have prayed to forget I have remembered. He loves me, he loves me not. Once I stood in a field of somebody else's flowers and had my way with them. Now I've got a man but ain't got no way to have with him or without him. Mammy hated when I talked that way. But I knew that language too. It comes back to me now. Surrounds me now in this Capital City. Now I have a man and a house, but my house has no garden. I don't know where the wild flowers grow 'round here. I have no way to know. And I don't know how I would know. I possess no way to know. None at all.

And I can't recall how to tell a curing from a killing herb.

He has interesting memories that trot out to me in well-turned phrases, my Congressman. His smile is quick. He has the habit of charm. He is a public feast that is gnawed daily, not my private meal. What would I not give for a corner of this bread to call my own? That's easy. My freedom. This feeling I call "free" I would trade for nothing. Not one thing. And I don't even know good what it is. What it is. But I know I saw it, like a crack of light coming in under the door, saw it in the Congressman's eyes. Felt it tingling on the places on my arms he touched while we danced. Feel it in the circle of the dance. Around again and around again till everything collapses or disappears. I felt that free-y feeling in his arms. Now we slither around the ballroom. Am I the invisible feet of the snake? Or am I the horse prancing?

Did I know right then what it was, or was it the moment later? The moment when R. tapped the Congressman's shoulder, waited imperiously for the Congressman to step away, then pulled me closer, like a shackle snapping on my wrist, felt the hand that had signed the paper to buy me caress the nape of my neck. Just as the feeling was escaping, I could named it, free-y. But it was gone, and that old familiar feeling, that comfortable feeling, of being possessed came to me. We danced something gallant, in the old lazy high-stepping way. The Congressman walked away and off the dance floor; the Negro man walks away. R. and I are left on this dance floor become a stage. This is our cake walk. Everybody looks at us high-step.

63

The Confederate and his quadroon. Redeemed I was, I was sold and he bought me. I should let him be my God; I have let him be my God. He redeemed me and I have loved him for it. Where do I go, to go and sin no more? The Congressman walked away, arm in arm with some young dark lady, the gap-toothed girl. He walked away as R. twirled me on my aching toes.

64

I am trying to remember; but I don't know what I have forgotten. I wish I had run down the road alongside Other toward Mammy. I wish Other had got there first but Mammy kept looking down the road for me. I wish Other looked up to Mammy with pleading eyes. I wish I arrived at Mammy's knee. I wish Mammy bent over and lifted me from my feet. I wish Mammy kissed me as Other watched. I wish Mammy loved me and Other saw it.

But that's never going to happen. She's dead now. She's dead, and all I think about is not her and where she is and what she is now; I still think only of her and what I want and what I missed. Look at me this way. They always say we don't have family feelings. I hate proving them right. When I lived with the white people in Charleston, I used to cry out loud for my Mammy just so they wouldn't think I didn't care that I was torn away and stole. I wanted them to know I felt something. And I did feel something. Just not something for her. My cry was a lie.

I liked R. right from the first. He was good-looking and tender almost and he was funny in a biting way. And he could always see how strange life was, how it was what you loved that bit you, how it was the thing you lost and scrambled to find that killed you, how you were always doing the almost exact opposite of what you needed to do to be happy. He could laugh at the way life was folded, almost exactly on top of itself and upside down. He was, he is, a deeply and easily amused man who didn't think life meant anything, who wasn't afraid of God, or beholden to God, or grateful to God, or mad at God. He didn't seem to think at all on God and consequently didn't mind that God didn't think on him.

All of this drew me in like fresh clean water. I was so tired of talking to God. It was good to talk to R. He talked back, and he fucked, and he kissed. He was better than God; then he was my God. He taught me how to read and write, and it was as if he created me. I started writing and it was just like he took a rib from my chest and created a partner for me. Adam had Eve and I have pages. My pages are my Eve and they are my Cains and my Abels and the generations descended from Adam. I liked R.—sure enough. Liked him the way I liked God. I admired him and wanted things from him. I took my little petitions to him and they were answered.

I didn't start loving him until he saw Other. I didn't start loving him till he wanted her and me, but wanted me more. I didn't start loving him till he preferred me to her. Oh God, I loved him then. So much was reconciled for me in his reach for my nipple before her breast, my kiss before her breath, so much reconciled and so much redeemed, forever reconciled and forever redeemed.

And now it's coming unraveled. What if Mammy always loved me, and loved me more? What if Garlic was right? What if Lady was black and loved me and loved me more? What if I had never lost the first race? What does that do to the savor of the second? Why was I all the time looking over R.'s shoulder at the Congressman walking away from me? Why was the Congressman walking away with a dark lady? Why am I not considered the most beautiful woman in the Capital City? How much longer shall I stay here?

65

R. came to me last night and I could not move myself to turn toward him. In my mind I said, "Hand, reach to him"; in my mind I said, "Leg, raise up and drape on him." In my mind I moved to caress him in all my old ways, but my body didn't move. He waited for me as he sometimes does. I am twenty-nine years old. Or am I thirty-one? For fifteen years he has come to me quickly and directly or still and waiting. Never exchanging touch for touch as we did in my dreams. He touched me, or I touched him. Tonight he lay waiting, and I found no way to touch him. He closed his eyes and said to me, Et tu, Brute? Et tu? Then he told me the story and we were back to the days I was fifteen and he was just over thirty; he was young and I was younger; he was teacher and I was student; yes, he told me of Caesar and the friend who betrayed him, the last one to stab him, and we wrestled like bears in the bed, arms grabbing arms, rolling around in the bed, laughing, because this is what we loved, him teaching me, and me touching him. It was good for us, that. Good and gone, like the wind done gone.

66

The Congressman stopped by to discuss something with R. When I carried in a decanter, the Congressman seemed to be studying the angels dancing on the toe of his boot. He didn't meet my eye. R. smiled on me fondly and took the decanter from my hand. When the door was closed, I could hear R. laughing. If the Congressman made a sound, you couldn't hear it on my side of the door. I would have liked to stay and visit. But it wasn't mine to linger without invitation. I went upstairs and started sorting clothes, first mine, then his. Those are the jobs that remain to me, the ones that require discernment.

R. is having the house packed up. He wants to sail for Europe. London to begin. One of the colored girls from Nashville spoke to me of London. She sang there, or hoped to sing, for the Queen—is that how it was? Or had she already done it. Queen Victoria, who took sides against the slave trade, short and squat with lots of babies. I would like to see Buckingham Palace, and the Thames River, and the white cliffs of Dover again. I would like to see something more than the dark Mississippi or the lingering Potomac. He says we'll leave from New York. But I am not leaving for New York. I'm looking for the words to tell him that I wish to remain in the Capital City.

67

*S*oon it will be Easter. I like the preacher at my Washington church. I can walk to the church from our townhouse. He was enslaved in Mississippi. He came to Washington looking for a wife he had lost before the war. He had been sold down the river into Louisiana, but he heard his wife had made it into Georgia, then up into Washington, so he came here. Truly, it was not the wife he was looking for, but the children, who had gone with the wife. He loved him some children, that man did, loved him some children. Around Atlanta he tired of looking.

My Congressman has never been married. Rosie sews a little for his sister. Rosie says his sister "always be after him 'bout marryin'. 'Specially when dis young friend of hern come by. She ain't 'xactly a pretty girl, but they say she, Corinne, be real smart. She wear these round gold glasses and she got a neat-enough figure, just ain't much to it. But they say she went to Mount Holyoke, passin', for a year, and that's supposed to be somethin'. She graduated from Oberlin." Rosie says the Congressman say, "A man who can't protect a woman ought not get married." She say his sister say, "If you can't protect a woman, no colored man in this country can." The Congressman don't answer that. At least not so Rosie can hear. I'm wondering what his answer is.

After the war my preacher got baptized and came up to Washington. He's real easy on the eyes and not so hard on the conscience. The old ladies like it when he comes to call. I can't wait to hear him preach Easter Sunday. I'll wear my new hat.

68

I have had a life, and all of it is divided, but not like the newspapers up North say.

When I saw R. in his army uniform, it killed something in me. Even now, when he lies naked in my bed, why do I sometimes see those brass buttons on him, see them when I don't want to see them? Why do I touch the little knobs on his chest and pull them like pulling the brass off his jacket? When I see the brass on the jacket, why do I hear coins jangling in my father's pocket?

All Daddy counted was acres. All Other counted were the coins. All I count is the slaves, trying to get the number down to ought. Always ending up with one; sometimes it's Mammy and sometimes it's me. There always seems to be one of us who don't want to be free.

69

*T*hings are not easy for my Congressman. There are Negroes in the Congress now and one or two in governors' mansions, but the tide is turning. R. doubts my Congressman will be re-elected. I fear he will lose his seat at my table as well as his seat in the Congress. If R. has no use for him, he'll find no place for him. It would be beyond the breadth of R.'s imagination or the length of his eyes to see our friendship. To give the devil his due, if R. saw our friendship he might stir a breath to protect it. He is not a man lacking in generosity. But you can't protect what you don't see. The Congressman will lose our house with his seat.

I didn't read the papers till I came to this city. I have been a farm girl even when I was a farm girl living in town. All I knew were the people on our place, the land, the sky above, the crop, and dreams printed on paper and bound in leather covers. Here the dreams walk and talk, eat and spit. The world comes to me. Comes to my table for dinner, invites me to tea, sits by my pot while I drink my morning coffee. I who didn't know till days after the war had begun or until days after the war ended. Now I sit in the shadows of those making the news of the day.

Reconstruction has been under attack from the moment it was born. The Klan is on the rise and increases in its violence. No one knows how long we coloreds will keep the vote. The Freed Men's Bureau is overrun with people who can't read or write, who don't know how old they are or where they were born, but are looking for somebody—a wife, a mother—whose name they cannot spell, whose age they do not know, whose state of residence they do not know. These are the people I lend money to. I know the time and day I was born. Mammy made Lady write it down.

Lady told me that. When I traced her neat script with my finger, she quickly tripped along, "Your mother worried me from the moment you came, to get that inscribed in the Bible." Mammy wanted the day and the exact time. "I told her," Lady said, "I thought the day would do, but Mammy wanted the time, and we don't own the exact time anywhere here on this plantation."

I am twenty-nine years old. He is forty-six. I have no words to tell him that I am not traveling with him to London. I have lived under his roof almost half my life, and the only other people who have provided me a roof are dead. I will go to London with him.

Tonight when he lies beside me I will reach for him before he reaches for me. I have half my life before me, and I cannot afford for him to grow bored.

70

The trip to London has been postponed, indefinitely. We are leaving for Nashville! I will see Jeems. R. has some connections in that city. A maiden aunt with a bit of fortune and an awkward assemblage of hangers-on, threatening to bleed her whiter than she already is. Folk in Charleston think he should have gone as soon as possible, and the letter was delayed in the post, so he needs to leave already. He wants to travel light—without me, and this is a thing I would have accepted. It is our usual way for me to stay at home, stay in our little enclosed world, but coming to Washington has changed that, and I have no taste for staying put. He tells me that people will know I'm his mistress—if I go.

I tell him, "Everybody I know knows I'm your mistress. It's only some of your friends who don't know. And can that matter to you now? Now, you think on marryin' me?"

"Precisely, my dear," he says. "I can't take you as mistress where I may one day want to take you as wife."

I shake my head and insist. I would like to stamp my feet. I have no taste for being separated from him now. "Don't you have friends in the city with whom I can stay?" He doesn't seem to be giving it a thought. So I say, quietly, "Some of the old folk from Cotton Farm live in

Nashville. Write to the family at Belle Meade. Ask them to let me stay in one of the old cabins. All things can be arranged between gentlemen."

"I am surprised you'd be willing to stay back in the cabins."

"Why? Lincoln freed the slaves. What do I have to worry about?"

"It's been a long time since you were in the cabins."

I let him pull me into his arms. "I'd do more than that for you."

He kisses my head and agrees to write the letter. "I feared you were succumbing to the charms of Washington," he says.

Hope of visiting Jeems makes me nostalgic for spacious, high-ceilinged rooms and lavish plaster embellishments. The outer doors, the front doors of Tata were six feet wide. When they were open, it was as if the side of the house had been taken down. We will take back this place, we will take back this place, a tree once grew where this dining room stands and will grow there again; we will take back this place, nature says as you move through the house; and it was Garlic who created the structure that said it.

Later, I take a nap and dream of Jeems.

71

The carriage ride to Belle Meade is not to be. Me be, we be, I am, we are sailing to London. We are sailing to London. I am and he is, the sail and the wind, and the old city. We are a whisper of wind seeking for London, a clean rag from the wash on a straight-up pole, pushing on to London. We are these new people who sail for pleasure. But the wind and the whisper and the rag are part of what I know, and the me in the other we, I am, fears. We are a sailed people. We sailed to America. We taste the path of our abduction in our tears. It's as if the house is on fire and I've got to get out quick.

Hate or fear of "crossing the water" may be the only thing I have left of my mother's, my grandmother's. Surely, it's the only thing that I have that I know I have. Maybe I have something else and I don't know it. If the fear were truly mine, I could touch it more intimately, get into its crevices, or let it get into mine, and I would know it. This feeling hangs down low in me, a heavy lump of an unexplored thing, like a clod of brown-red mud giving off some old mother heat.

The old aunt died before we could pack for Nashville. I long for forest. I yearn for the trees and the horses of Jeems, the steam from their nostrils and the steam from their fresh dung. I miss the safe inland cities. Nashville,

Atlanta. These cities with their front porches on the ocean, Washington, Savannah, Charleston, scare me, like a door left open on a dark night with robbers about.

But I am hungry for the city on the Thames. I think of the palaces, Hampton Court where Queen Elizabeth lived, I think of the Tower of London and all the things I read about in those Walter Scott novels and those slow Jane Austen pages. The only one of those I ever loved at all was *Mansfield Park*. Fanny hated slavers. I think of all those ladies now because—why? Because—why? Because, having forgotten what I saw there, they are all I know of the world to which I am going. Dusty pages. Mouse supper.

72

I laughed so hard at breakfast, my insides got tickled. I laughed so good, I was the giggle and I was drunk on it too. I laughed so hard this morning my stomach hurt from stretching and shaking. The deep belly laugh cures more than you know that ails you. I had forgotten that. It's been so long since I had one. The rumble and the jiggle of the thing does a woman more good than a poke. But the good strong belly laugh is harder to come by than a good stiff poke.

Debt Chauffeur, that's my name for him now, wants to marry me. He asked me down on bended knee, and I would have been honored — except he wants us to live in London, and he wants me to live white. I crowed at that. I laughed so hard, and not a tear came. He couldn't understand it. I don't often think on how white I look; it's always been a question of how colored I feel, and I feel plenty colored. He said that no one in London will know that I'm supposed to be colored. And I said I am colored, colored black, the way I talk, the way I cook, the way I do most everything, and he said but you don't have to be. She was "black" and she didn't seem it, and she was not that much lighter than you, and she was "black."

At last that explained everything to him. I understood it near at once. It had never seemed before that he so little knew me. Always at least he knew the difference between her and me, and now he saw little difference, and the advantage was all to Other.

I tell him. Mammy is my mother. I think of her more as the days pass. I can't pass away from her. He says she's the one asked me to do it. I don't believe him, and he hands me another letter.

73

The script was ornate but the words were crude. I didn't recognize the handwriting. Before I read the contents I guessed the fine script belonged to some Confederate widow, a general's wife or daughter, who owed a favor to Lady and repaid it to Mammy. But what I read Mammy would never have dictated to any friend of Lady's. I suspect she came to Atlanta, came to Atlanta and didn't visit me, came to Atlanta and got someone from the Freed Men's Bureau to do her writing. I can hear her saying, "Git it 'xact. I ain't here fo' no about." Syllable and sound, the words were Mammy's.

Dear Sur,

You done already send one of mah chilrens back to me broke. Lak an itty bitty thang, a red robin, you done twist her soul lak da little neck and huah can't sang no mo'. She was mah Lamb, so I guess that how that goes.

Now you got mah chile. What was my vary own. Dat's a love child you got, Cinnamon. Skinny as stick, spicy and sweet. An eyes-wide-open-in-the-daylight child. She need a rang on her finger and some easy days, dat gal do. I had me the roof and the clothes, I watch huah Lady wear de jewels but Ah ain't neber cared nothing about dat. Ah done toted and tarried and twisted mah own few necks, but dis ain't about dat. Let mah child love you. And let Gawd love her too. For what I done for you little Precious. Yo' chile dat died. Marry mah little gal.

    I am sincerely,

    Her Mammy

Beneath the last two words Mammy had placed her mark, a cross in a circle.

74

I cried enough to ride back to Africa on a slide of tears. "Mah little gal"—what I wouldn't give to hear her speak those words I see on the paper; what I would not give does not exist. I want to eat the paper. I would give anything to hear her say "mah little gal." What am I writing? I would give everything to hear her say anything at all. I want Mama, I want my mother. I want Mammy. It's easy to want her, now that I know she wanted me. If I coulda wanted her when I didn't know she wanted me, she might be mine right now. She might be alive right now. Mammy never stood foot on London. Ah ain't goin' dere. I ain't goin' nowhere she ain't been. I'm staying here and looking for what's left of her.

75

$\mathscr{D}$ebt says all that's left of Mammy is me. He is polite enough to flinch as he says it. I ask him if he's imagining me fat and dark. He don't answer. He tells me about a dream Other used to have. A dream of hers. She was lost in a fog, running, looking for something, and she don't know what. Other never knew what she wanted, so she never had it even when she did. I ask him why he's still talking to me about her when she's buried in the ground. I say I know what I'm looking for. When I was a little girl I was looking for love. When they sold me off the place I was looking for safety. At Beauty's I was looking for propriety, and now, and now I have drunk from the pitcher of love, and the pitcher of safety, and the pitcher of propriety till I feel the water shaking in my ears. But thirst still burns. What I want now is what I always wanted and never knew—I want not to be exotic. I want to be the rule itself, not the exception that proves it. But I have no words to tell him that, and he has many feelings for me, but that is not one of them.

Later, I look at my reflection in the glass—and I try to see what he sees. I look for the colors. I see the blue veins in my breast. I see the dark honey shine of my skin, the plum color of my lips. I see the green of my eyes, and I see the full curve of my lips and the curl of my hair, and I know that it's not so very bad being a nigger—but you've got to be in the skin to know.

Am I still laughing? It is not in the pigment of my skin that my Negressness lies. It is not the color of my skin. It is the color of my mind, and my mind is dark, dusky, like a beautiful night. And Other, my part-sister, had the dusky blood but not the mind, not the memory. There must be something you can do or not do. Maybe if the memories are not teased forth, they are lost; maybe if the dance is not danced, you forget the patterns. I cannot go to London and forget my color. I don't want to. Not anymore.

76

I had never known him to be ignorant. But he is. He thinks like the others, the common tide. He thinks that the blackness is in the drop of blood, something of the body. I would have thought he knew enough women's bodies to know that that could not be true. And enough blacks and whites to know there is a difference. What did I suck in on Mammy's tit that made me black, and why did it not darken Other's berry? Was there some slight tinge, some darkening thing about Other? Lady's fortitude; Other's willingness to take to the field? And how does one explain the sisters except that part of the blood memory must be provoked and inspired and repaired, time and again, to become the memory.

This tied-up-in-ribbons gift I want from him, he has no picture in his head of what that gift looks like unwrapped. No picture at all. The lift of a hat, the dip of his back—those gestures would remain as they have been, but the bitter curve of his lip holding back a laugh that salutes all that is strange and lacking in harmony in me, in him, in us, would vanish. That curve in his lips, that spark in his eye of—truth—yes truth, there is so much in me strange and discordant. The notion of respecting me, as me, myself, would be, is, half foreign to his mind. No, no, not foreign; foreign is this coming week of travel, that idea is not foreign to him. Respect for me is foreign to me. Respect for me is an accomplishment of his, mine by gift, not mine by right. Absence and exoticism are such different keys of longing. He adores me, he has worshipped me, I believe he loves me, but never could the tone of his feeling be formed so that this cautious emotion, this sturdy food, "respect between equals," be what you called the way his heart turned toward mine.

It was always some warmer feeling, not the cold distance of temperance. I want his respect. I have fragments of it and fractions. He admires my mind. I have read more books than any woman he knows well. The way I break rhythms, the way I make rhythms, he yearns for the music of my way of telling, of being, of seeing. But now our love songs are played in two keys: grief and remorse. I prefer grief to remorse. Without mutuality, without empathy to join and precede sympathy, I am but a doll come to life. A pretty nigger doll dressed up in finery, hair pressed for play. I will be the solace of sorrow but not the solace of shame. I have been dropped too deeply into the shame bucket to borrow any that belongs to somebody else. I wrap my shame in his respectability, I let his arms wrap 'round my shoulders, his weight press me into a sense of place. His self plunging into my heart awakens me, and, with it, a weak humiliation I've known so long, an aching bruise it pleasures to touch.

And yet and still I have wanted this for a long time. It was my first woman's dream. I have wanted this for too long to walk away without the prize I have coveted. I will marry him. I will marry him. I believe I will marry my Debt.

I read what I have written, and I wonder if I am not deranged. There is such a distance between the words and the events. And a greater distance between my feelings and the events. My feelings are closer to the words. I have never felt close to the events, because I have never controlled them. Someone else has written the play. I wish I could think it was God. I merely take my place on the stage. I wish whoever was writing the action would send the Congressman to call.

77

If I will not play the role in London, Debt sees no reason for us to quit the country. If I am to remain colored, I can remain colored just as easily here. According to him! I don't believe colored is easy anywhere. But I'm pleased to be spared the sea voyage. Again I remember stories from the quarters when I was young and stories from the docks in Charleston, stories of men and women and children chained into the bowels of ships. I hear them crying down the century. There is a song that came from the ships. I heard the story. The slaves sang some old tune and the ship was lost at sea. The owner was a slaver from way back and deep in his soul his conscience clean. But the ship got caught up in a storm where storms don't come, and he thought he saw the hand of God when the lightning cracked in the darkness. And he prayed to God to save him. And God spoke to him. God said, "I ain't saving you ifn' I don't save the ship. And I ain't saving the ship lessen I save the Daddys, and I ain't saving the Daddys without the Mammas and I don't need the Mammas less I save the babies. You is less to me than spit. But if I save the babies, I'll save the Mammas." And God saved them all, and the man did not forget, Amazing grace! How sweet the sound of the slaves singing that saved a wretch like me. He once was lost but now he's found, was blind but now he sees. That happened to an Englishman; let it happen to me. Please Lord, let me see what it is that I want.

78

I woke up this morning and some strands of my hair were on my pillow, the red butterfly was on my face, and my bones ached where they came together, like somebody was splitting kindling on me, and I am tired. I am shaking when Rosie comes for a fitting; she gives me the address of an old conjure woman born herself on African soil who lives just on the east side of the Capitol building. The conjure woman tells me to lie down in a dark room, and I do. I'm like one of those creatures from the swamp, one of those ghosts who only ride at night. I sleep in the day and come out in the darkness.

Debt says we are to marry before we go home. I am too weak to say anything but yes.

79

*T*oday was my wedding day. Strangers stood up for us. I believe they played Mendelssohn's wedding march.

Rosie sewed my dress and didn't say a word. It was the golden color of sweet cream. When R. slipped the gold band onto my finger, I thought, I wish this had happened a long time ago—when I was still in love with Planter, when I still begrudged her every kiss she had off him. We return to Cotton Farm for the wedding trip. He says, "We should be home for Christmas." Where does he think that is?

80

*T*ata rises from the middle of Cotton Farm surrounded by its fields of sorrow. It is hard to get out of the carriage in this territory of truth and illusion.

The wide front doors are flanked by windows—sidelights, we call them. Over the door is the half-circle of a red Venetian glass fanlight; the diamond-shaped muntins surrounding the front door hold blue glass. "Muntins"; Lady taught me that word. I was born in a world of colored light and flickering shadows. I was born in the kitchen of a great house.

81

Garlic was waiting at the door. Outside it, really. He had on just his own new clothes, but he stood ramrod straight, as he had in his old before-the-freedom livery. After dinner Debt ceremoniously gave me the keys to the house, the house he had inherited from Other. Later that night Garlic took them from me. "Did you dream of this when you first came here?" I had to ask him that. Age had not stooped him. But when he stood with a hand tucked inside his shirt, it brought to mind Mr. Napoleon Bonaparte. "What didn't we dream of?" he responded. "What didn't we dream?"

82

We took supper in the dining room. Debt was irritated by every manner of small thing. He squinted at the bright light coming through the window where no curtains hung. And we shivered in the cold. "I'll burn this place to the ground it we can't get things 'round here the way they need to be for folks to live in it," R. roared. Garlic said, "Gold damask would suit the room well, sir." I agreed, and R. approved the funds for this and other renovations.

Some things were the same—the cool tile floor, alternating diamonds of light and darker gray, and, outside, a planting of periwinkle, a small evergreen vine that bears blue flowers, the scent of periwinkle and flowering almond reminding me of when I was his Cinnamon and she was his coffee.

83

I visited the cemetery today. I stood over the grave of my mother, then of my half-sister; I stood over the grave of my father, Planter. And then I knelt at the little boys' graves, the graves of his sons. Shall I always wonder if my mother and Garlic killed those children? And will I ever know? I asked Garlic directly, and he answered, "If we didn't, it was because we didn't have to." Sons would have challenged Garlic's authority over the house. "I wonder what problems I pose to you?" I asked. "None at the present time, none at the present time," he said. Then he stopped and pulled out my father's watch, the one Other had given him. His finger released the mechanism, and the face was revealed. His finger snapped the watch shut. "If you had been my child, this place would be yours, now, yours." Why did it seem so plainly Garlic's to give and take away? I wondered who had planted the tree just up from the gate, the tree that killed Planter when he smashed into it. I wondered how long some folk can watch and wait.

84

*C*hristmas is coming. In the old days we'd be looking for the Yule logs now. The white folk thought there was only one—as long as the Yule log was burning, it was Christmas and nobody was whipped and nobody really worked 'cept those in the house. That was our hard times: when the house was full of guests needing cooking and looking after all the night, even the night before Christmas, but it was good foods and smells for kitchen folk too, and the field folk had a holiday by taking their rest. While the Yule log burned, things were different. So one log burned in the big house and another burned way out in the quarters. Out there somebody tended the ghost fire, burning the second log and maybe a third, to within an inch of the big house log—an inch bigger, an inch longer—but something close to it. We would trade the bigger log for the smaller. That way we kept Christmas longer.

The year I turned twelve the Twins, Other's big-boned, red-haired Twins, came up to the house for a big dinner before leaving on a winter's hunt. Jeems was with them. No one went to bed till late. The night was cold and quiet. The stars so still and lovely, until they began to cry out and awaken me. I slept beside Other on the floor of her room. I got up, pushed open the window, and stared out like a wolf cub. That is exactly how I felt. Young, dangerous, like I could loot a henhouse on my paws with my teeth. Frisky, like the moon was lifted into the sky to listen to me howl. Like I could bite anyone and eat anything and leave my piles wherever I pleased. That night I felt that way. Everybody should have one night like that sometime in their life. But you pay the high price. If you have one, you'll want another, and maybe never get it. Yearning is a heavy purse. But not to know is a lighter, more starving, burden. Me, I carry the weight of knowing, cuddling close the hope I will know again what I have known before. I stood out there. Opened my mouth and howled. I made no real sound. Only a high-pitched sob no one heard, a squeaking whine that came from the soup of sky and earth and time spinning inside me. I looked out into the darkness and saw Jeems looking across his own darkness hearing me. His teeth and eye whites shined so bright into my darkness, I got scared. I stuck my thumb in my mouth and began to suck. I ran back to my piece of the floor, curled into a little ball, and rocked myself to sleep. It was Christmas Eve.

85

$\mathcal{C}$hristmas Day came and went. Plum pudding, goose, just us. No one from the neighborhood. No one Debt is willing to know is willing to know me. I believe that the count in the community is he has gone to crazy. When Debt got up from the table to go into Lady's old office, a room I am changing into a library of sorts, I asked Miss Priss and her parents to join me. Garlic carved from the joint and we all ate well.

Today is New Year's Day. I am too tired to write most of the time. Downstairs they're cooking black-eye peas. It supposed to bring good luck. I'm not eating any black-eye peas. Nothing no black people are doing in any large number is bringing good luck to anybody. We ain't got no good luck. I won't eat any black-eye peas. Maybe I'll eat the greens, though. Garlic eats greens every first of the year, and in a way he is a rich man. Maybe the greens work, less folks do it. Maybe it works; some of us are getting over.

This place, every inch of it, feels like a tomb. I can't wait to get back to Atlanta.

86

*W*e are leaving today. And I think back on the first time I left this place for good. Planter say, "You the devil yourself, child."

"How you know that?" I ask.

"Every time I look at you I feel the devil inside me. Your Devil calling to my devil to get out."

"How you get him back in when he come out?" I ask.

"I drown him in whisky," my Daddy says.

"How'm I gonna get my Devil back in?" I ask Daddy.

"I don't know, child, I don't know. What I do know is there's nothing for you on this place, child, nothing but vinegar. I'm not waiting for the day my daughter's husband takes her sister to his bed. It's done everywhere over this county, but it won't do here. Side by side to my Miss, she will suffer in the comparison, and you will suffer if I leave you here to watch her marry." He said all that. It was all mixed up and halting. But he got it out after a time.

I got mine out quickly, at last. "You could set me free."

"It is better be a slave to a rich man than a slave to poverty. Poverty is a cruel master, a cruel master every day. And there are kind masters in the world."

"I don't want to go."

"You distract your mother more than you know. And I have lost too many children for her to lose none."

"What has that to do with me?"

"I'm willing to lose another to make her feel the loss of one. My sorrow needs company."

So he sold me to his friends in Charleston with the promise they would be kind, and they were kind enough. But the influenza came through, and so many died in so few days, so many wills, and I was passed along with the Thomas Elfe chairs from house to house, until, like the chairs, I stumbled into an establishment more starved of cash than elegance, and I was sold. Too many folk died, and I was in the market and my breasts were turning red from the sun. Later, the skin from my chest would come off in sheets. This is my story and I tell it again.

———

I get in Debt's carriage. It was an altogether different girl that got into Planter's then. Back then, before the country was at war, when the belles were still dancing, and the swains still provoked swooning, when the blue blood of the South was huntin', shootin', fishin', drinkin', arguin', and even studyin' a little, at Virginia, at Princeton, at Harvard, and at William and Mary, before the first public brother-against-brother blood had been publicly shed, I went to war, and I was a battlefield.

My weapon against fear was anger. My shield against pain was my own screamless, bloodless, battlefield surgery performed without ether or alcohol. I cut off memories, I gouged out feelings the way you gouge out the little dirty places on a potato you dig up in the field before you serve it at the table. I gouged out dirt holes where I found them in my soul, and in my mind, and in my heart. I amputated and cauterized with searing thoughts, thoughts so disgusting I not only never thought them again, I recollect distinctly I have never thought again in the particular place that spawned the particular thought. And with the bleeding parts cut away, the necessary places cauterized, I survived, as fortunate soldiers do.

I fought my war before the war. And in it I earned my courage. And when I stopped being afraid, there were not many places left to hurt, and I thought so fast and clear—so separate I was from feeling. Feeling slows down most women's minds. Mine is not hindered like that. It is not burdened.

I think quick. So I recall it's not slavery and freedom that separate my now from my then; it's when I could read and when I could not, it's when Mammy loved me and I didn't know it, and when Mammy loved me and I did. It is when Lady was white and when Lady was black. It is still me, and it's still a carriage, but me in the carriage has changed more than I would have thought possible. All my old dreams have come true, and I am too tired to dream anew.

Other's man, house, and farm are mine; this is not a

complete surprise. These things were hoped for and achieved. To look in the mirror and know, not simply that my beauty eclipsed hers, but that it is elemental, that it does not require purchase or contrast to be, or to be valued, is a miracle. A miracle begun when? When I saw myself reflected in the Congressman's eyes as I twirled in his arms. I want to see myself, again, in that mirror.

87

We are back in Atlanta. It seems so short and flat after the Capital. A place to move through, not a place to stay. A place that was not, a place that will be, but a place of friends. This is the only city in the world in which I have friends. Am I am ready to rest and be thankful?

88

I tiptoe into Beauty at breakfast this morning. Just looking at her makes me smile. She powders her face so white and dyes her hair so red, I expect to hear God shout down, "So you think you paint better than me!"

"Mrs!" Beauty says out loud to me. I hold out my hand

and wiggle my finger; the ring sparkles. She presses a cup of coffee into my hand and I too sip. "I wasn't jealous of you having him in your bed. I had that before you did, but I don't believe anybody's ever married me. I think I'd remember if they had." We both laughed.

"I know you've been asked," I say.

"Asked, yes, I've been asked but not by him, and he's the only one I'd give up my ladies for. For him and a proper ring, I might just have given up pussy."

"You are too horrible," I say. If I could be scandalized, I would be.

She hugs me. It's a way of saying congratulations, well done. She kisses me on the forehead and I kiss her on the lips. I am so tired of being alone, and Debt has not been true company for me in a long time, since before Precious died. We are just old times now. I kiss Beauty because Jeems is a glorified stable boy and the Congressman is far away and because we both love R. One way of looking at it, all women are niggers. For sure, every woman I ever knew was a nigger—whether she knew it or not.

We dip toast into our coffee, and it is sacrament, bene- diction, and prayer.

I go home and pray for more.

89

*T*he Congressman sent his card 'round to me. I waited for him all the afternoon, and he did not come until evening, when R. received him and I sat in the drawing room keeping busy, not with my sewing but re-reading this diary. The men caught me at it. The Congressman feigned snatching it away. Mr. Chauffeur assured him that the sanctity of the little book would never be violated under his roof. The Congressman commended R.'s virtue, and I contradicted him. He possessed not virtue in surfeit, but curiosity in deficit.

90

*B*eauty and I were out in the shops together this afternoon. We passed the Congressman, and he lifted his hat and bowed in my direction. There was a sober look on his face and a smile of complete contentment that provoked restlessness in me. I want to taste what he tastes.

91

I am feeling a touch poorly. My joints are aching almost all the time now, and I must be clever with my hair; I've lost quite a bit of it. There is a doctor in Washington I particularly like. I've asked R. to make arrangements for me to see him. There's worry in R.'s eyes. His worry makes me worry more.

92

R. has asked the Congressman to accompany me back up to Washington, as he is going in that direction and R. is tied by business to this city. The Congressman has further suggested that I stay at the home of his sister, a Mrs. Harris who lives in Le Detroit Park near Howard University. I am alarmed to be so happy. Later, R. told me that he was touched by the Congressman's kindness and would seek to do business with the man even when he wasn't in office. "Some of them are rather fine sorts of men," R. says. "Not the finest, but fine."

93

The train has the same effect as a draught of laudanum. It excites and numbs at the same time. The *shake shake shake* of the wheels under you quiets the spirit, the monotony of sound quiets the soul, and the ever-changing scenery occupies the mind simply. Nothing remains in view long enough to hold on to. Another way of sleepwalking with your eyes wide open.

The Congressman doesn't dance attendance on me, but he makes his presence known. He brings an extra pillow, a glass of water, a cup of coffee. This morning when he offered the coffee, he allowed his fingers to brush over mine. It was the first time we had touched since we danced.

"Perhaps you'll take me dancing while we are in the Capital City," I venture.

"I don't think my fiancée would like that."

"I'm not sure that I like that you have a fiancée."

The Congressman laughed at that, big guffaws.

"Why are you laughing? Was she the gap-toothed girl you danced with after you danced with me, the last time we danced?"

"Yes."

"Had you asked her then?"

"No, then I was thinking of asking you."

I blushed; my cheeks, my breast turned scarlet. "You hoped I'd marry you?"

"Yes. Given the choice between being my wife or his mistress, I thought you might choose — wife."

"You should have asked me."

"If I had known how soon the opportunity would vanish, I might have done something different. I don't imagine you would prefer being my mistress to being his wife."

Sleeping on the train is like riding a horse. Except you don't feel the wind; you see it. Things pass you by so quickly, until you realize that things are not passing you by; you are passing by the things, the trees, the ponds, the people. The people don't pass you by; you pass them by, carried along by power you don't see, carried along on a track you didn't create, and there is no way of getting back to any one pretty piece of property. You are moving too quickly. And you are old enough to know that anything you have time enough to get back to, has time enough to change before you can get back to it. You are sad.

I want to get up from this bunk and go to him. I have more imagination than he. I can close my eyes and want to be that which he cannot imagine me preferring to be. I can prefer to be different than I am now. The worm does not imagine becoming a butterfly, but I have seen the worm and the butterfly, so I don't have to imagine.

Does the worm die and the butterfly is born where the worm was, or is it a continuous life, without stops? Or is it no life at all without thought, or memory, or an ability to cry out loud? Possessing only beauty, is the butterfly alive? I'm too tired to chase after my mind as it rambles. More in the morning.

94

*M*orning came, and I came crisp and clear with it. We are pulling into Washington soon. I must put you down to stroll these kinks out of my legs.

95

*B*etrayer! I leave you down and you tell him what I have whispered into your pages. I came back, and there he was, reading, intent on his reading.

I said, "Sir, you are no gentleman!"

He said, "You're right about that, *Cynara*." He knew my name and called me by it. "I'm a man." He teased me, and it was infuriating. "A strong man, a statesman, a colored man, but I am proud to say I am no gentleman."

I spoke the verbal equivalent of a foot stamp. I pouted like the schoolgirl I had never been instead of the whorehouse maid I was. I couldn't stop myself from saying, in all petulance, "All the years I lived under his roof, he had respect for my privacy!"

He could only just stop himself from laughing at me. "No, you got that just about right the first time. He had respect for privacy; it's a gentlemanly principle and you were the beneficiary. He didn't have respect for you—respect for Negro women is not a tenet of the code of the Southern gentleman, but it's a tenet of mine."

A silence fell between us that I didn't get the measure of.

Time was freezing or expanding; it was doing something to get me and keep me lost. I can't tell you if it was the longest minute of my life or the shortest hour, but I was lost in it. When I found myself, I reached out for my book. He held you out toward me like bait. I reached for you, pulled you toward me, felt him holding on, then relinquishing. I seized you.

"Thank you," I said as formally as I could manage.

He was trying to look right into me. "Don't thank me until you know I read it all."

"You didn't have time to read it all," I snapped back. I didn't know what he had read. But whatever he had read, he was looking at me with sharper interest. It is thrilling to be known even when the knowledge is stolen, stolen like rubies.

A price above rubies. A virtuous woman is worth a price above rubies. I was a maid untouched when I came to R., and she, Other, was not. She had had two husbands and two babies. I pride myself on being the only colored gal I know who's had only one man and no children. I suspect the stream of my passion is so powerful because I have shored it up so narrowly. No diversions, no creeks, no tributaries of any kind, have been allowed. This man before me could change all this.

I "merit a price above rubies." Were those R.'s words the night he bought me? What can those words mean to me now, today, to a woman pulling into the B & O depot accompanied by a Congressman? I was pleased that the train was pulling into the station. We had things to do other than the things I wanted to do, and I was pleased for that. He told me, in a tone that rude people reserve for servants, that we had many preparations to make before getting off the train. In a curt tone I never use, I suggested that he get on about it. Looking as if he wanted to slap me, he called for a servant and withdrew. Being careless with my packing, I stole time to write in you, traitor.

96

We traveled to his sister's in the northwest quadrant of the city in a hired carriage and in silence. We had never been so alone before. I had never been so alone with any man aside from my Debt. It was exciting to be so close and to withhold—everything. I am the river, and I am the dam about to burst. I will win if my walls hold strong, I will win if my passion burst through; either way is victory. I have never been in this position before in my life; either way I turn, I win. Until now my virtue has been unreal—never tested. Now in this man I have a true desire and a true question; the pleasure is exquisite. Exquisite; this is the wash of freedom. It has nothing to do with politics or elections. It has to do with having many things you want and being free to choose between them or free not to choose and remaining safely the same.

A Negro woman who would not change her position. This is a novelty. We have not liked where we were, even when we didn't know what or how to change, when we simply dreamed of flying away, I'll fly away, I'll fly away, when I die. But I imagine flying away into his arms, dying to be reborn again, and dying again and again, waking after each little death into new pleasures. But it is not imagining; it is remembering from long ago with the faces changed. I am a maiden no longer. We arrived at his sister's house without speaking a word. But his eyes told me, his eyes told me, he saw me beautiful, and my whole self told him, I hear you, and I like so very much what I hear.

97

*S*he wasn't there. The whole family was out. He showed me to my room, and I took my hat from my head, pulling out the pin; then I loosed my hair from the tight ball that was making my head ache. I turned back toward the door; he was looking at me, a suitcase in each hand. His sister does not keep servants. I walked toward him but only in the sense that a piece of metal jumps toward a magnet. I was drawn. I was pulled. I took my suitcases with my own hands from his, turned my face toward his, opened my mouth wide. I waited for his lips. It was a wanton gesture. The first wanton gesture of my life. A gesture I had scorned when I had seen it in the whorehouse. He did not disappoint me. Lord, he did not disappoint me at all.

98

I have done what I would not have done had I contemplated it longer. I'm terrified. Moving to being a woman of his, I have found myself in the neighborhood of Beauty's girls, the women with more than one man. And then it is nothing at all like that or anything else I have known, this exquisite chaos.

This is what the psalmist was writing about in the Song of Songs. I recognize it at once. And I am afraid, not of his finding out, but of being this new person, a less than perfect person who has violated one of her most dearly held principles, and a person who has never felt such pleasure, a person I have never read about in books.

The pleasure of his body and the pleasure of his knowing me has carried me into some sacred territory I did not know existed. The mystery of making love to myself, for he is me, and I am he, and I know all that he and she want. In the church of this sex I am the preacher and the congregation. He is the preacher and I am the congregation. I am the preacher and he is the congregation. The call becomes the response and the response the call, and I am shouting and falling out. Eager to let the old Cinnamon die and let the new Cynara be born all the nights to come.

This is a sweet thing, sweeter than anything I have

ever known. If there is anything better than being a free nigger on Saturday night, it's being a free Negro on Sunday morning; in his sister's bed I have my cake and eat it too.

99

*W*e strolled out and about in the neigborhood later, easily arm and arm. No one much knows me up here. Many bob their heads, as if to say what a handsome couple. This is a new experience for me, but it is a familiar one for him. I don't have to ask him to know that he has never in his life touched a white woman, would not dream of kissing one, and that if he did dream of it, it would be an act of defiance, not of desire. It is less comfort, much less comfort, to realize he has an eye for all the chocolate, and the caramel, and the coffee-colored beauties on these streets, sashaying out to enjoy their freedom. He likes to look at pretty women; he allows himself the luxury of resting his eyes on their faces. I let my elbow find its way into his ribs.

"God wouldn't a made women so beautiful if He didn't want men to take a moment to enjoy the beauty He created! Lord knows you women don't care enough about your own appearance to be peeking in any mirrors."

I laugh at the silliness he wraps around some of his sharper truths. I am the only dark woman R. notices. I should find comfort in that fact but it—discomfits me.

Many folks recognize the Congressman, men in overalls, men in hats; he treats all alike and bows to them slightly. If there's a baby in arms, he threatens to kiss it, then shakes his head, walking forward and announcing, "Too much innocence for me to taint."

R. is a rich man and perhaps a powerful one. My Congressman is a famous man and perhaps a powerful one. I'm beginning to discern the differences and how they might matter to me.

100

He asks me about my sister, Other. I have nothing more to say. I am bored with that story. Today is the day I go to see the doctor. There is no one else for him. The girl I saw dancing with him so long ago is an old friend of his family he might have married had he not met me.

101

*T*he doctor, one of the first colored doctors in the country, had not very much to say—except he's seen my butterfly before and with it the aches in the bone—but there are other things I do not feel and that make him hopeful. He says the tired comes and goes. He says sometimes people die. He says I'm lucky I didn't have a baby, because sometimes that makes it worse.

Through this all he was more reserved than he had been before. Quite a bit more reserved. In fact, it took a few days for me to get the appointment. Finally, after the examination, when I was dressed and about to leave, he cleared his throat and said what I believe he had been trying to say all the while.

"Madam, when I first met you I was impressed by your deportment." (I would rather he had said intelligence and simple grace.) "You were in a difficult position, but you handled yourself with modesty. (I would rather he had modified the modesty perhaps by adding simplicity, humble modesty.) "All eyes could see that you were in the best and the worst sense of the word married. But you bore the yoke with…" (Did he call it grace?) "When you married, we were happy for you. Every Negro man who had a mother forced or cajoled by the master raised a cup to your victory. But now you come to town with no husband, only an intent on sullying the good name of one of the great dark men in the Capital City. I can't but join my fellow citizens in disapproving."

"I don't think you know anything of my situation."

"I can smell him on you."

It was the most vulgar sentence I had ever had spat at me. I know what he meant. I had washed the linen at Beauty's. Being a doctor is another kind of washing of the bedsheets.

"He will never be elected again if he keeps up with you. Voting Negroes won't vote for a man living with an-other man's wife." I tried to interrupt him, but he wouldn't be stopped. "Whoever you think you are, in the polite society of Negro teachers and preachers and lawyers and doctors, you will always be the Confederate's concubine." He was on a roll. "You have a greater chance of being accepted among old white families than new col-ored ones." And he kept on going. "We're a prim and proper lot."

I hadn't thought of this. I hadn't thought of very much at all.

102

My business in Washington is complete. I should return by the first train to Atlanta. It would be the sensible thing to do, and I am a sensible woman. No lady in any novel I know makes the kind of mistakes in books that I make in life. In all the literature I know, only one book comes close to what I feel. This is *Great Expectations*. Pip has a guilty family. Almost guiltier than mine. What is owed the rescuer? Do we always fall in love with those who rescue us? Didn't I know Miss Havisham in calico? What don't Estella and Other have in common? How easily Pip accepted his good fortune. I envy white boys that most of all—their certainty that they're going to be or get lucky. It occurs to them to live with great expectations. It occurs to them to do what they want and not worry about it. It occurs to R. to do that all the time. It doesn't occur to me at all. It occurs to me to run back to Atlanta.

103

R. has moved back into Other's house. Her children are there, and they need him. There's the grand staircase he once carried her up—and too many rooms to count.

This is where we huddled together when Precious died.

He sends a card 'round to my house, and I arrive at the appointed hour for my visit. We make love. He traces the butterfly on my cheek. And he asks if I am going to be all right. I tell him yes—and I tell him that I'm leaving him in the morning. In the morning, I'm leaving him. I've just made up my mind to do it. When I said it, I was letting him know how unhappy I am. Now I'm hearing myself. I'm leaving in the morning.

"I gave you my name," R. says.

"I never told you mine," I reply.

104

*M*ammy never rode the train. I've got Lady's emerald earbobs in my purse. I took them from Other's jewelry box. Some folks say emeralds are higher than peridots because there are more peridots in the world. It's what's scarce is high. Some folks say it's because emerald got a prettier color. I say it's because the rich folks found emeralds first and have more of them, so they say the peridot be just a little better than green-colored glass to give higher value to what they have a higher number of. Like white blood. But a man made the green-colored glass and God made the emerald and the peridot, and I can't help knowing the peridot is the pretty color of grass in the fall, the color of living things that survive the thirst of late summer when there's so much gold in the green. I see the peridot and the emerald are the same beautiful thing, and green glass is something altogether different.

I'm riding on the train up to Washington, alone. I don't send word ahead. No. All I have taken out of his house are her things. I take her things and leave her—him. This is the best I can do with this algebra of our existence. She gets him, and I get her things. Everything he bought me I left behind, every pair of bloomers, every barrette, the peridot earbobs, the wedding ring, everything. I cannot go to my Congressman in R.'s things.

I went up to her room. I opened the closet: a sea of green, velvet, satin, silk; a gown or two in black; a blue day costume; hats. It was said around Atlanta that she liked green best because it is the color of money. But I who knew her from the first day either of us knew anything, knew that she loved green before she even knew what money was.

You don't see paper money on a cotton farm. You don't even see paper money on what it was and I have not wished to claim, a great Georgia plantation. On a place like that, in the place we lived together, half-sisters separated by a river of notions: notions of Negroes and notions of chilvary, notions of race and place, notions of custom and rage; in the country we inhabited in our childhood, you measured wealth in red earth and black men. There was nothing green in it.

Green were the leaves, green was the grass, green the grasshoppers, green all the insignificant pretty things, all the moving tokens of living, and that's why Other loved green, because she was, or saw herself to be, an insignificant pretty living thing. She didn't wear it because of the money or because it matched her eyes. She wasn't, in fact, vain. She knew I was the prettier one. Knew it right off and didn't let it worry her.

She wasn't pretty, but she had the capacity to distract men from noticing that. And now that my looks are vanishing with the years, I must borrow that from my sister; I must learn to make men not notice that I am not beautiful. Her dresses are a fine beginning. I will go to my Congressman in my sister's clothes.

I packed in her trunks. I look at my reflection in the window and it's a blurry thing, but I see me as I have never been before. I wear green well. For somehow, too, green is Daddy's Ireland.

Garlic told me the story. He got it from Mammy, who had got it from Planter. Planter ran out of Ireland with the law on his tail, wanted for a murder he had committed. And thieving he had thieved. He couldn't see other people have everything when his family had nothing. And when things were too hot in that country, he quit it. That was her father and that was mine.

She was like him in that she killed. Miss Priss told me that story. She, Other, and Mealy Mouth killed the Union soldier, robbed his dead body, and dragged him off in their chemises, all the while making light conversation with the family out the window. I come from a strong people. And I am like him in my willingness to leave my world to find a better one. It is a sister and a family I leave behind, not Other, not some thing.

Once in Georgia I had a sister who loved my mother dearly; she took care of Mama all her life, better care of her than I took. I hated her and buried her, and now I forgive her. Once in Georgia I had a mother I could not find my way to loving. I'm grateful that Other found a way and kept the path clean and brightly used. She made exquisite use of my mother's love.

And now it's my turn to make good use of her mother's love. Lady loved her black man in the bright light of day. If he will have me, I will love Adam, I will love my Congressman that way.

105

$\mathscr{R}$. writes me letters it would bore me to return. He is someone else's dream. Whose dream I'm not sure. I suppose Beauty's. Beauty stretched the scope of her imagination to see him, to want him. She didn't like men, but she loved him. That's tribute. Other loved him when she had nothing else to love. It was a scrawny little pathetic love, and he wouldn't have it. And me, I loved him because he was the prize, and I wanted the prize to feel and know, taste and see that I could win it, but it was his power I craved, not him.

I tell him, I have been sleeping in my sister's bed. I don't want that anymore.

He tells me, I saw you before I ever saw her, wanted you before her.

But then you chose her because you could and she reminded you of me. She was your daylight version of me. You betrayed me and I betrayed her on so many succulent occasions, too many succulent occasions. But I no longer have a taste for that meat. It's too rich for me. I want something simple, like a cold joint of ham, a slice of cornbread, and a big glass of buttermilk. I want to love a stranger who knows no one I know. You have been a father to me, and now that you look the part, I don't want you. His eyes well up. I won't give you a divorce. I'll live in sin. Proudly. You taught me that.

"What is your name," he asks me.

"Cynara," I say, walking out his door.

106

I am traveling unescorted. I feel nauseous. There are rascals of every hue on this train. Whatever remained of my good name will be gone by the time we reach Washington. Why doesn't anyone assume that a woman on her own wants to be?

The Congressman doesn't know I'm coming. The election is fast upon him; he doesn't need anything more to worry him. He can't imagine I will come.

R. imagined I would go. He sent a note 'round to my house. I call it my house because he gave it to me, because my name is on the deed, and because, as Beauty says and it's ugly to admit, I earned it.

R. wrote to say that if I was going to Washington, I could stay at "the house." He doesn't say my house, and he doesn't say ours. His kindness makes me cry. I am touched that he knew, could figure out, what I would do; his kindness makes me cry, but I can't accept it anymore.

107

*T*hough I had money, they wouldn't rent a hotel room to an unaccompanied woman. I hired a driver to take me to my Congressman's sister's house. When she opened the door she remembered me.

108

There is a ball tonight at the university. All the great Negro leaders of the city will be present. The election has come and gone. My Congressman will be Congressman no more when they swear in the new House. His sister has invited me to go with her party to the ball. I have things to tell him. I hope I can find the words.

109

We danced tonight. But before we danced I made preparations.

I had the slim gap-toothed girl, Corinne, over for tea. I suspected three or four things about her, one or two of them very important to me. Her flat chest and narrow hips reminded me of Mealy Mouth, only more. It was not easy issues I sidled up to, but I sidled up under the guise of sharing the story of a girl cousin who was married but rocked an empty cradle. She never swelled. The girl shrugged.

Her teeth were pretty, really, little pearls with a tiny little part in the middle of her smile. She was unashamed; things were as God intended them. If she was to live alone, well, she wasn't alone; she was with her parents. And she had the children in the settlement houses. There was important work to do and she was doing it. She knew how much the Negro population had increased since the end of the war. How many more hungry stomachs and hungry minds. How little helpful political currency remained. "Odd," she said, making a delicate joke to change the subject, "my female trouble is that I have no female trouble."

She took the bitter with the sweet and swallowed them both whole. "The only man who should marry me is a widower with five children who need someone to raise them. He would be lucky to get me."

"What about the Congressman?"

"He wants a family. He kept talking to me about babies, and that's when I pulled away."

"You love who you love," I say.

"You're blessed with whatever you're blessed with."

"Wherever it comes from."

"We're not in very different boats, are we?"

"You could not be more wrong," I say. Of a sudden I am frozen. After all these years she could not be more wrong.

If I find a way to offer my gift, will she find a way to accept?

110

I pressed crushed flowers into the hem of my dress and into its creases. Scent rises in waves from my garment as I move. I tell him that he must marry the gap-toothed girl. He laughs. We dance more. He pulls me deeper into the dance; we swirl, and I am drunk on the power that is flowing out of his body back into our country, our America. I look around me at these new Negroes, this talented tenth, this first harvest, the brightest minds, the sustained souls, the ones so beautiful they have received some advantage, and so strong they need not what they did not receive. Folks whose fathers were named Fearless and were freed because their master was afraid to own them. The ones who could intimidate from shackles. These beautiful ones. They are as close to gods as we have seen walk the earth. I dance and I see them dance in the darkening night as clouds roll in, covering the stars that shine upon the ones who survived the culling-out of the middle passage, and the mental shackles of slavery; the group that rose with the first imperfect freedoms to this city, to the Capital, this group of Negroes shining brightly as their—as our—flame burns down as our time passes.

This short night they call Reconstruction is ending. We dance in our twilight, and I know it. It is a secret greater than the secret I carry. Once in north Alabama rose a brilliant black man who no one gave a chance at all, rose and rode to Washington to take his place in the Capital City, a man who stole a woman from the oldest, richest family in the Confederacy. I saw that man. I saw him in the company of the nation's finest men, and I saw him stand toe to toe, and he was taller. But he is leaving the District of Columbia soon, and I don't know how long I will be around. I get too tired to remember. We swirl, the old fiddle sings us tunes, and when he pulls me closest, I tell him he must marry the girl and why. This is our Götterdämmerung. This is the twilight and we are the gods.

111

The Congressman married the doctor's daughter; that's what the town said. The girl who attended New England Female Medical College. In a little African Methodist Episcopal church. I was the only witness.

I sold Lady's earbobs and bought a little house out by the water in Maryland. Its weather-darkened bricks are from before the birth of our nation; the woods that sur-round my place are older still. The Frederick Douglasses are talking about buying some nearby property and building a home. When the time comes, I think I will be ready for neighbors. If and when the Douglasses come, they want to encourage others to migrate with them. It's starting to be hard times for Negroes in the city, and it's always been hard times for Negroes in the country. It's easier to live where fewer dreams are buried.

112

A son has been born to the Congressman, a legitimate heir. A beautiful, beautiful boy. He came into the world so pale, his mother fretted for days over his little Moses crib, praying for a little dark to come in. There were good signs from the start, a bit of brownness 'round his cuticles and the tips of his ears, but like many light-skinned babies his eyes are a greeny-gray. I am to be the Godmother. They named him Cyrus after me. I took him back to an Episcopal church to be baptized; I couldn't wait for the Baptist immersion. If anything happens to my Godchild, I want him to go straight up to heaven and wait for his father and mother. I want no doubts at all.

113

Oh, my goodness. He is here. I call him Moses. I'm keeping Cyrus for his Poppa and Mama today. I tell him the story of Moses. I hold him above my head and I tell him about the mother making the cradle and setting it to float in the bulrushes. I tell him about the woman who put him in the cradle and the woman who found him. Some folks say she was the same woman, some folks say she was not. I know both women loved the baby. I am not so very well now. I think about the old days some now, and for the very first time I understand something about Mealy Mouth. The very best days are the days on which babies come. I'm so tired, I forgive her for what she had done to Miss Priss's brother, beat until he bled to death because something he said about a time he had had with Dreamy Gentleman. And I forgive Miss Priss for what she done to Mealy Mouth. And what that done to Other. And what that done to me. The very best days are the days the baby comes.

114

This is for you, my darling, emperor of the Congress of my heart. For you, Adam Conyers. Congressman Adam

Conyers of Alabama, self-educated trained to the bar. I had intended to get a job on the new Negro newspaper. I had intended to write about the ladies and the parties they gave and the dresses they wore. I had intended to make you and him proud of me. All my life I saw the tangles that stood between me and love—until you. When I saw you, I refused to see the tangles, and I stubbed my toe, got swoll up and burst, and now it looks as if I'm going to die.

I have never felt so loved as the day we waited for the baby's color to show or not show. And I knew because you told me, and I believed what you said, that you knew who the Mama was, and that was good enough for you. Anything of mine you loved. And lucky for me he's yours; it's been hard for me to love anything of mine. But just in time, loving what belongs to you means loving my own.

Tell your son all of this—when he's grown. Tell my Moses. Don't let it form him, and he will grow strong enough to master it. Shield the child from the truth of shackles, and no shackle will hold the man. The bars that cannot be broken are behind the eyes; the whippings you can't survive are the ones you give yourself. Let respectability be his first position; then nothing on this earth can shame him. Tell him his mother bought that respectability with lonely blood, and it is his birthright. Tell him that I was the chosen witness of the twilight, of you, my God. Ask him to pray against his mother's blasphemy. Tell him if we are as a people to rise again, it will be in him. Tell him I only did one great thing: I bore a little black baby and I knew—what every mother should know and has been killed out of too many of my people, including my mother—I bore a little black baby and knew it was the best baby in the world. Tell your wife, tell my gap-toothed Corinne, a lifetime of hating Other has made me fit for an eternity of loving her. Tell them both, I learned to share in peculiar circumstances. Now, the wind done gone, the wind done gone, the wind done gone and blown my bones away.

---

the End

POSTSCRIPT

Cindy, née Cynara, called Cinnamon, died many years later of a disease we now know to be lupus. She left her entire, not inconsiderable, estate to Garlic. She left her diary to Miss Priss, who left it to her eldest daughter, who left it to her only daughter, Prissy Cynara Brown.

The Congressman's son, Cyrus the first, never made it back to Congress, but his grandson, Cyrus the third, did. Today, Cyrus represents a district near Memphis, in Tennessee. He married a Nashville girl who practices law to support her horseback riding. They named their first-born son Cyrus, Cyrus the fourth, but added Jeems in honor of one of her ancestors who had helped train the first American grand national champion. Little Jeems, as he is called, has his eyes on the White House.

Cotton Farm still stands just outside Atlanta. Jeems's christening, upholding long-standing tradition, occurred in its great hall, overlooked by an oil portrait of Garlic that Debt Chauffeur had painted just before he died. In his will, Debt left Cotton Farm, fallen on bad times and in disrepair, to Garlic, with the wish that he rot with the farm until he died and rot in hell after. Many thought R. just wanted some good company. Garlic used Cynara's money to repair the place.

When Garlic died, he left his pocket watch to the Congressman's son, along with half of Cotton Farm. The other half he left to Miss Priss, of course!

The mortgaged farm supplied the funds for Cyrus the third's successful election to Congress.

Like Mammy, Lady, and Planter, Cynara, Congressman, and Corinne were buried together. For all those we love for whom tomorrow will not be another day, we send the sweet prayer of resting in peace.

ACKNOWLEDGMENTS

Caroline is my strongest inspiration. I would burn this book unpublished if it would ensure her happy life. She would pull it from the fire; my daughter is a brave and generous soul.

Mimi has proven herself to be my life's longest sweet companion. David is the redeemer of my faith in romantic love; his history is my future. Jun is our Godfather. Anton is my best book friend. David F. is my longest friend-boy. Jane is Sunday afternoon. Ann is my magnolia blossom. When I had very little else, I had Marc and in a different time Marq. Happy Birthday, Joan B. and Judge Cliffie. Bob G. and Edith and Michael believed in me from the beginning. Roberta was my beginning. The Smiths embody the best of Cotton Farm—home. Gail sparkles. Forrest helped me see, Somers helped me survive. Jed is the brightest person I have ever known, still. Grandma is Grandma, and Sonia is our Aunt. Lea is

Godmommy. Kimiko is my sister. And Flo is my shero. Ricky carried the ashes. The Congressman owes much to Reggie. And Jerry is my Garlic. Courtney sang. Quincy brought me to the big show. Brandon I miss. George I think on every day. Their love sustained my creativity.

And a blessed thanks to Kazuma, Charlie, Moses, and Lucas, my Godsons, and Takuma, Caroline's Godson, whose very existence lit the last turn of this book toward its ending.

Margaret Mitchell's novel *Gone With the Wind* inspired me to think.